RUDY A
BABE1

OR, THE CAPTURE OF THE
EAGLE'S NEST

Hans Christian
Andersen

CHAPTER I.

LITTLE RUDY.

JET us now go to Switzerland, and see its wonderful mountains, whose steep, rocky sides are covered with trees. We will climb up to the fields of snow, and then make our way down to the grassy valleys, with their countless streams and rivulets, impetuously rushing to lose themselves in the sea. The sunshine is hot in the narrow valley; the snow becomes firm and solid, and in the course of time it either descends as an avalanche, or creeps along as a glacier. There are two of these glaciers in the valleys below the Schreckhorn and the Wetterhorn, near the long village of Grindelwald. They are a remarkable sight, and therefore many travelers from all countries come in the summer to visit them: they come over the high mountains covered with snow, they traverse the deep valleys; and to do this they must climb, hour after hour, leaving the valley far beneath them, till they see it as if they were in an air-balloon. The clouds hang above them like thick mists over the mountains, and the sun's rays make their way through the openings between the clouds to where the brown houses lie spread, lighting up some chance spot with a vivid green. Below, the stream foams and blusters; but above it murmurs and ripples, and looks like a band of silver hanging down the side of the rock.

On either side of the path up the mountain lie wooden houses. Each house has its little plot of potatoes; and this they all require, for there are many children, and they all have good appetites. The children come out to meet every stranger, whether walking or riding, and ask him to buy their carved wooden châlets, made like the houses they live in. Be it fine or be it wet, the children try to sell their carvings.

About twenty years since you might have seen one little boy standing apart from the others, but evidently very desirous to dispose of his wares. He looked grave and sad, and held his little tray tightly with both hands as if he was afraid of losing it. This serious look and his small size caused him to be much noticed by travelers, who often called him and purchased many of his toys, though he did not know why he was so favored. His grandfather lived two miles off among the mountains, where he did his carving.

He had a cabinet full of the things he had made. There were nut-crackers, knives and forks, boxes carved with leaves and chamois, and many toys for children; but little Rudy cared for nothing so much as for an old gun, hanging from a rafter in the ceiling, for his grandfather had told him it should be his own when he was big enough to know how to use it.

Though the boy was little, he was set in charge of the goats; and Rudy could climb as high as any of his flock, and was fond of climbing tall trees after birds' nests. He was brave and high-spirited, but he never smiled except when he watched the foaming cataract, or heard the thundering roar of an avalanche. He never joined in the children's games, and only met them when his grandfather sent him to sell his carvings; and this employment Rudy did not much like. He would rather wander alone amongst the mountains, or sit by his grandfather while he told him stories of former ages, or of the people who lived at Meiningen, from whence he had come. He told him they had not always lived there, but had come from a distant northern country called Sweden. Rudy took great pride in this knowledge; but he also learnt much from his four-footed friends. He had a large dog, named Ajola, who had been his father's; and he had also a tom-cat who was his particular friend, for it was from him he had learnt how to climb.

"Come with me on the roof," the cat said to him; for when children have not learnt to talk, they can understand the speech of birds and animals quite as well as that of their father and mother; but that is only while they are very little, and their grandfather's stick seems as good as a live horse, with head, legs, and tail. Some children lose this later than others, and we call them backward. People say such funny things!

"Come with me, little Rudy, on the roof," was one of the first things the cat had said which Rudy had understood: "it is all imagination about falling; you don't fall if you are not afraid. Come; put one of your paws so, and the other so! Feel for yourself with your fore-paws! Use your eyes and be active; and if there's a crevice, just spring and take firm hold, as I do!"

Rudy did as he was told, and you might often have seen him sitting beside the cat on the top of the roof; afterwards they climbed together to the tops of the trees, and Rudy even found his way to the rocky ledges which were quite out of the cat's reach.

"Higher! higher!" said the trees and the bushes; "see how we can climb. We stretch upwards, and take firm hold of the highest and narrowest ledges of the rocks."

So Rudy found his way to the very top of the mountain, and often got up there before sunrise; for he enjoyed the pure invigorating air, fresh from the hands of the Creator, which men say combines the delicate perfume of the mountain herbs with the sweet scent of the wild thyme and the mint found in the valley. The grosser part of it is taken up by the clouds, and as they are carried by the winds, the lofty trees catch the fragrance and make the air pure and fresh. And so Rudy loved the morning air.

The happy sunbeams kissed his cheek, and Giddiness, who was always near, was afraid to touch him; the swallows, who had built seven little nests under his grandfather's eaves, circled about him and his goats, singing: "We and you! and you and we!" They reminded him of his home, his grandfather, and of the fowls; but although the fowls lived with them in the same house, Rudy had never made friends with them.

Although he was such a little boy, he had already traveled a considerable distance. His birthplace was in the canton of Vallais, whence he had been brought over the mountains to where he now lived. He had even made his way on foot to the Staubbach, which descends through the air gleaming like silver below the snow-clad mountain called the Jungfrau. He had also been to the great glacier at Grindelwald; but that was a sad story. His mother lost her life at that spot; and Rudy's grandfather said that it was there he had lost his happy spirits. Before he was a twelvemonth old his mother used to say that he laughed more than he cried, but since he had been rescued from the crevasse in the ice, a different spirit seemed to have possession of him. His grandfather would not talk of it, but every one in that district knew the story.

Rudy's father had been a postilion. The large dog, which was now lying in the grandfather's room, was his constant companion when traveling over the Simplon on his way to the Lake of Geneva.

4

Some of his relations lived in the valley of the Rhone, in the canton of Vallais. His uncle was a successful chamois-hunter and an experienced guide. When Rudy was only a twelvemonth old his father died, and his mother now wished to return to her own relations in the Bernese Oberland. Her father lived not many miles from Grindelwald; he was able to maintain himself by wood-carving. So she started on her journey in the month of June, with her child in her arms, and in the company of two chamois-hunters, over the Gemmi towards Grindelwald. They had accomplished the greater part of their journey, had passed the highest ridge and reached the snow-field, and were now come in sight of the valley where her home was, with its well-remembered wooden houses, but still had to cross one great glacier. It was covered with recent snow, which hid a crevasse which was much deeper than the height of a man, although it did not extend to where the water rushed below the glacier. The mother, while carrying her baby, slipped, fell into the cleft, and disappeared from sight. She did not utter a sound, but they could hear the child crying. It was more than an hour before they could fetch ropes and poles from the nearest house, and recover what seemed to be two corpses from the cleft in the ice. They tried every possible means, and succeeded in restoring the child, but not his mother, to life; so the old man had his daughter's son brought into his home, a little orphan, the boy who used to laugh more than he cried; but he seemed to be entirely changed, and this change was made down in the crevasse, in the cold world of ice, where, as the Swiss peasants think, lost souls are imprisoned until Doomsday.

The immense glacier looks like the waves of the sea frozen into ice, the great greenish blocks heaped together, while the cold stream of melted ice rushes below towards the valley, and huge caverns and immense crevasses stretch far away beneath it. It is like a palace of glass, and is the abode of the Ice-Maiden, the Queen of the Glaciers. She, the fatal, the overwhelming one, is in part a spirit of the air, though she also rules over the river; therefore she can rise to the topmost peak of the snow mountain, where the adventurous climbers have to cut every step in the ice before they can place their feet; she can float on the smallest branch down the torrent, and leap from block to block with her white hair and her pale blue robe flying about her, and resembling the water in the beautiful Swiss lakes.

"I have the power to crush and to seize!" she cries. "They have robbed me of a lovely boy whom I have kissed, but have not killed. He now lives among men: he keeps his goats amid the hills, he ever climbs higher and higher away from his fellows, but not away from me. He belongs to me, and I will again have him!"

So she charged Giddiness to seize him for her, for the Ice-Maiden dared not venture among the woods in the hot summer time; and Giddiness and his brethren—for there are many of them—mounted up to the Ice-Maiden, and she selected the strongest of them for her purpose. They sit on the edge of the staircase, and on the rails at the top of the tower; they scamper like squirrels on the ridge of the rock, they leap from the rails and the footpath, and tread the air like a swimmer treading water, to tempt their victims after them and dash them into the abyss. Both Giddiness and the Ice-Maiden seize a man as an octopus seizes all within its reach. And now Giddiness had been charged to seize little Rudy.

"I seize him!" said Giddiness; "I cannot. The miserable cat has taught him all her tricks. The boy possesses a power which keeps me from him; I cannot seize him even when he hangs by a branch above the precipice. I should be delighted to tickle his feet, or pitch him headlong through the air; but I cannot!"

"We will succeed between us," said the Ice-Maiden. "Thou or I! I! I!"

"No, no!" an unseen voice replied, sounding like distant church bells; the joyful singing of good spirits—the Daughters of the Sun. These float above the mountain every evening; they expand their rosy wings which glow more and more like fire as the sun nears to setting over the snowy peaks. People call it the "Alpine glow." And after sunset they withdraw into the snow and rest there until sunrise, when they again show themselves. They love flowers, and butterflies and human beings; and they were particularly fond of Rudy.

"You shall never catch him—you shall never have him," said they.

"I have captured bigger and stronger boys than he," said the Ice-Maiden.

The Daughters of the Sun now sang a song of a traveler whose cloak was carried away by the storm: "The storm took the cloak but not the man. You can grasp at him, but not hold him, ye strong ones. He is stronger, he is more spiritual than we are! He will ascend above the sun, our mother! He has the power to bind the winds and the waves, and make them serve him and do his bidding. If you unloose the weight that holds him down, you will set him free to rise yet higher."

Thus ran the chorus which sounded like distant church bells.

Each morning the sunbeams shone through the little window of the grandfather's house and lighted on the silent boy. The Daughters of the Sun kissed him, and tried to thaw the cold kisses which the Queen of the Glaciers had given him, while he was in the arms of his dead mother, in the deep crevasse, whence he had been so wonderfully rescued.

CHAPTER II.

GOING TO THE NEW HOME.

RUDY was now a boy of eight. His uncle, who lived in the Rhone valley at the other side of the mountains, wished him to come to him, and learn how to make his way in the world; his grandfather approved of this, and let him go.

Rudy therefore said good-by. He had to take leave of others beside his grandfather; and the first of these was his old dog, Ajola.

"When your father was postilion, I was his post-dog," said Ajola. "We traveled backwards and forwards together; and I know some dogs at the other side of the mountains and some of the people. I was never a chatterer, but now that we are not likely to have many more chances of talking, I want to tell you a few things, I will tell you something I have had in my head and thought over for a long time. I can't make it out, and you won't make it out; but that doesn't matter. At least I can see that things are not fairly divided in this world, whether for dogs or for men. Only a few are privileged to sit in a lady's lap and have milk to drink. I've never been used to it myself, but I've seen a little lap-dog riding in the coach, and occupying the place of a passenger. The lady to whom it belonged, or who belonged to it, took a bottle of milk with her for the dog to drink; and she offered him sweets, but he sniffed at them and refused them, so she ate them herself. I had to run in the mud beside the coach, and was very hungry, thinking all the time that this couldn't be right; but they say that there are a great many things that aren't right. Would you like to sit in a lady's lap and ride in a carriage? I wish you could. But you can't arrange that for yourself. I never could, bark and howl as I might!"

This is what Ajola said; and Rudy put his arms round him, and kissed his cold, wet nose. Then he took up the cat, but puss tried to get away, and said, —

"You're too strong! and I don't want to scratch you. Climb over the mountains, as I taught you. Don't fancy you can fall, and then you will always keep firm hold." As he said this, the cat ran away; for he did not wish Rudy to see that he was crying.

8

The fowls strutted about the room. One of them had lost its tail feathers. A tourist, who imagined he was a sportsman, had shot its tail off, as he thought it was a wild bird.

"Rudy is going away over the mountains," said one of the fowls.

The other one replied, "He's in too great a hurry; I don't want to say good-by." And then they both made off.

He then said good-by to the goats; they bleated "Med! med! may!" and that made him feel sad.

Two neighboring guides, who wanted to cross the mountains to beyond the Gemmi took Rudy with them, going on foot. It was a fatiguing walk for such a little boy; but he was strong, and never feared anything.

The swallows flew part of the way with them. "We and you! and you and we!" they sang. Their route lay across the roaring Lütschine, which flows in many little streams from the Grindel glacier, and some fallen trees served for a bridge. When they gained the forest at the other side, they began to mount the slope where the glacier had quitted the mountain, and then they had to climb over or make their way round the blocks of ice on the glacier. Rudy sometimes was obliged to crawl instead of walking; but his eyes sparkled with pleasure, and he planted his feet so firmly that you would think he wanted to leave the mark of his spiked shoes behind him at every step. The dark earth which the mountain torrent had scattered over the glacier made it look almost black, but still you could catch sight of the bluish-green ice. They had to skirt the countless little pools which lay amongst the huge blocks of ice; and sometimes they passed by a great stone that had rested at the edge of a cleft, and then the stone would be upset, and crash down into the crevasse, and the echoes would reverberate from all the deep clefts in the glacier.

So they went on climbing. The mighty glacier seemed like a great river frozen into ice, hemmed in by the steep rocks. Rudy remembered what he had been told, of how he and his mother had been pulled up out of one of those, deep, cold crevasses; but he soon thought no more of it, and it seemed no more than many other stories which he had been told. Occasionally, when the men thought the path too rough for the boy, they offered him a hand; but he was not easily tired, and stood on the ice as securely as a chamois. Now they got on rock, and clambered over the rough stones; then they would have to walk through the pine-trees, or over pasture-lands, whilst the landscape was constantly changing. Around them were the great snow mountains — the Jungfrau, the Mönch and the Eiger. Every child knew their names, and, of course, Rudy knew them. Rudy had never before been up so high; he had never walked over the wide snow-fields: like the ocean with its waves immovable, the wind now and again blowing off some of the snow as if it were the foam of the sea. The glaciers meet here as if they were joining hands; each forms one of the palaces of the Ice-Maiden, whose power and aim is to capture and overwhelm. The sunshine was hot, the snow was brilliantly white, and seemed to sparkle as if covered with diamonds. Countless insects, most of them butterflies or bees, were lying dead on the snow; they had gone up too high, or been carried by the wind, and had been frozen to death. A threatening cloud hung over the Wetterhorn, looking like a bundle of black wool; it hung down, heavy with its own weight, ready to burst with the resistless force of a whirlwind. The recollection of this whole journey — the encamping for the night, at such a height, the walk in the dark, the deep clefts in the rock, worn away by the force of water during countless years — all this was fixed in Rudy's memory.

An empty stone hut beyond the *mer de glace* gave them shelter for the night. Here they found pine branches for fuel, and they quickly made a fire and arranged the bed as comfortably as they could. They then seated themselves about the fire, lighted their pipes, and drank the hot drink which they had prepared. They gave Rudy some of their supper, and then began to tell tales and legends of the spirits of the Alps; of the mighty serpents that lay coiled in the lakes; of the spirits who were reported to have carried men in their sleep to the marvelous floating city, Venice; of the mysterious shepherd, who tended his black sheep on the mountain pastures, and how no one had seen him, although many had heard the tones of his bell and the bleating of his flock. Rudy listened to all this, though he was not frightened, as he did not know what fear was; and as he was listening he thought he heard the weird bleating; it grew more and more distinct till the men heard it too, and left off talking to listen, and told Rudy to keep awake.

This was the Föhn, the blast, the terrible tempest, which sweeps down from the mountains upon the valleys, rending the trees as if they were reeds, and sweeping away the houses by a flood as easily as one moves chessmen.

After a time they said to Rudy that it was all over, and he might go to sleep; and he was so tired with his long tramp that he obeyed at once.

When day broke, they pushed forward. The sun now shone for Rudy on new mountains, new glaciers, and snow-fields. They were now in the canton of Vallais, and had crossed the range which could be seen from Grindelwald, but were yet far from his new home. Other ravines, other pastures, woods, and mountain-paths now came into sight, other houses, and other people; but they were strange and deformed-looking beings, with pale faces, and huge wens hanging from their necks. They were *crétins*, feebly moving about, and looking listlessly at Rudy and his companions — the women were particularly repulsive to look at. Should he find such people in his new home?

CHAPTER III.

UNCLE.

RUDY had now come to his uncle's house, and found to his relief that the people were like those he had been used to. There was only one *crétin*, a poor silly boy—one of those who rove from one house to another in the canton of Vallais, staying a month or two in each house, and the unfortunate Saperli was there when Rudy came.

Uncle was a great hunter, and also knew the cooper's trade. His wife was a lively little person, and almost looked like a bird; her eyes were like those of an eagle, and her long neck was quite downy.

Rudy found everything new to him—dress, habits and customs, and language, though he would soon get used to that. They seemed more comfortably off than in his grandfather's house. The rooms were large, and the walls were decorated with chamois' horns and polished guns, and there was a picture of the Virgin over the door; fresh Alpine roses and a burning lamp stood before it.

Uncle was, as I have said, one of the most successful chamois-hunters in the neighborhood, and also one of the best guides. Rudy soon became the pet of the household. They had one pet already, an old hound, blind and deaf; he was no longer able to go out hunting, but they took care of him in return for his former services. Rudy patted the dog, and wished to make friends; but he did not care to make friends with strangers, though Rudy was not long a stranger there.

"We live very well here in the canton of Vallais," said uncle; "we have chamois, who are not so easily killed as the steinbock, but we get on better than in the old days. It is all very well to praise former times, but we are better off now. An opening has been made, and the air blows through our secluded vale. We always get something better when the old thing is done with," said he; for uncle had much to say, and would tell tales of his childhood, and of the days when his father was vigorous, when Vallais was, as he said, a closed bag, full of sick folk and unfortunate *crétins*; "but the French soldiers came, and they were the right sort of doctors, for they killed both the disease and the persons who had it. The French knew all about fighting; they struck their blows in many ways, and their maidens could strike too!" and here uncle nodded at his wife, who was a Frenchwoman. "The French struck at our stones in fine style! They struck the Simplon road through the rocks; they struck the road, so that I may say to a child of three years old, 'Go to Italy, keep right on the highway!' and the child will find himself in Italy if he only keeps right on the road!" and then uncle sang a French song, "Hurrah for Napoleon Buonaparte!"

Rudy now heard for the first time of France, and of Lyons, a great town on the river Rhone, where his uncle had been.

In a few years Rudy was to become an active chamois-hunter. His uncle said he was capable of it; he therefore taught him to handle a gun and to shoot. In the hunting season he took him to the mountains, and made him drink the warm blood from the chamois, which keeps a hunter from giddiness. He taught him to know the seasons when avalanches would roll down the mountain sides, at midday or in the afternoon, according to whether the sun had been strong on the places. He taught him to watch how the chamois sprang, and notice how his feet fell that he might stand firm; and that where he could obtain no foothold he must catch hold with his elbows, grasp with his muscles, and hold with his thighs and knees — that he might even hold with his neck if necessary. The chamois were very wary, — they would send one to look out; but the hunter must be still more wary, — put them off the scent. He had known them so stupid that if he hung his coat and hat on an alpenstock, the chamois took the coat for a man. Uncle played his trick one day when he and Rudy were out hunting.

The mountain paths were narrow; they were often a mere cornice or ledge projecting over a giddy precipice. The snow was half melted, and the rock crumbled beneath the feet; so the uncle laid himself down at full length and crept along. Each stone, as it broke off, fell, striking and rolling from ledge to ledge till it was out of sight. Rudy stood about a hundred paces from his uncle on a projecting rock, and from this point he saw a great bearded vulture swooping over his uncle, whom it seemed to be about to strike over the precipice with its wings, to make him its prey. Uncle had his eye on the chamois, which he could see with its kid on the other side of the ravine; Rudy kept his eye on the bird, knew what it would do, and had his hands on his gun ready to fire; the chamois suddenly sprang up, uncle fired, the animal fell dead, the kid made off as if it was used to dangers. At the sound of the gun the bird flew away, and uncle knew nothing of his danger until told of it by Rudy.

As they were going home in the best of humors, uncle whistling one of his songs, they suddenly heard a strange noise not far off; they looked round them, and saw that the snow on the side of the mountain was all in motion. It waved up and down, broke into pieces, and came down with a roar like thunder. It was an avalanche, not over Rudy and uncle, but near, too near, to them.

"Hold fast, Rudy!" he shouted; "fast, with all your power!"

And Rudy clung to the stem of a tree; uncle climbed above him up to the branches and held fast, while the avalanche rolled past at a distance of a few yards; but the rush of air broke the trees and bushes all around like reeds, and cast the fragments down, and left Rudy pressed to the earth. The tree-stem to which he had held was broken, and the top flung to a distance; there, among the broken branches, lay uncle, his head crushed; his hand was still warm, but you would not know his face. Rudy stood pale and trembling; it was the first shock in his life, the first time he had felt horror.

It was late when he brought the tidings of death to what was now a sorrowful home. The wife was speechless and tearless until they brought the body home, then her grief broke forth. The unfortunate *crétin* hid himself in his bed, nor did they see him all the next day; but in the evening he came to Rudy.

"Write a letter for me! Saperli cannot write! Saperli can go with the letter to the post!"

"A letter from thee?" exclaimed Rudy. "And to whom?"

"To the Lord Christ!"

"What do you mean?"

And the half-idiot, as they called the *crétin*, cast a pathetic glance at Rudy, folded his hands, and said solemnly and slowly:

14

"Jesus Christ! Saperli wishes to send a letter to ask Him that Saperli may lie dead, and not the man in this house."

And Rudy took him by the hand. "That letter would not go there! that letter would not bring him back."

But it was impossible for Rudy to make him understand.

"Now thou art the support of the house," said the widow, and Rudy became so.

CHAPTER IV.

BABETTE.

WHO is the best shot in the canton of Vallais? Even the chamois knew. "Take care of Rudy's shooting!" they said. "Who is the handsomest huntsman?" "Rudy is!" said the maidens, but they did not say, "Take care of Rudy's shooting!" nor did their serious mothers say so either; he nodded to them as lightly as he did to a young girl; for he was brave and joyous, his cheeks were brown, his teeth sound and white, and his eyes coal-black and sparkling; he was a handsome fellow, and not more than twenty. The ice-cold water did not hurt him in swimming; he swam like a fish, could climb better than any other man, could hold fast like a snail to the walls of rock, for his muscles and sinews were good; and you saw when he leapt that he had taken lessons from the cat and from the chamois. Rudy was the surest guide to depend on, and might have made his fortune in that way; his uncle had also taught him coopering, but he gave little thought to that, for his pleasure and delight was in shooting the chamois; and in this way he earned money. Rudy was a good match, as they say, if he did not look above his own position. And he was a dancer among dancers, so that the maidens dreamt of him, and some of them even thought of him when waking.

"He gave me a kiss at the dance!" said Annette, the schoolmaster's daughter, to her dearest friend; but she ought not to have said that even to her dearest friend. Such a secret is not easy to keep: it is like sand in a bag full of holes, it will run out; and they all soon knew that Rudy had given her a kiss at the dance, though he had not kissed the one that he wanted to kiss.

"Just watch him!" said an old huntsman; "he has kissed Annette; he has begun with A and he will kiss all through the alphabet."

A kiss at the dance was all that the gossips could say against Rudy so far; but although he had kissed Annette, she was not the flower of his heart.

Down at Bex, among the great walnut-trees, close to a little rapid mountain stream, there lived a rich miller; his dwelling-house was a big building of three floors, with small turrets, roofed with shingle and ornamented with metal plates which shone in the rays of the sun or the moon; the biggest turret had for a weather-cock a glittering arrow which had transfixed an apple, in memory of Tell's marksmanship. The mill appeared fine and prosperous, and one could both sketch and describe it, but one could not sketch or describe the miller's daughter; at least, Rudy says one could not, and yet he had her image in his heart. Her eyes had so beamed upon him that they had quite kindled a flame; this had come quite suddenly, as other fires come, and the strangest thing was, that the miller's daughter, the charming Babette, had no thought of it, as she and Rudy had never spoken to each other.

The miller was rich, and his riches made Babette hard to approach; "But nothing is so high," said Rudy to himself, "that a man can't get up to it; a man must climb, and he need not fall, nor lose faith in himself." This lesson he had learnt at home.

It happened one day that Rudy had business at Bex, and it was quite a journey, for the railway did not then go there. From the Rhone glacier, at the foot of the Simplon, between many and various mountain-heights, stretches the broad valley of the Rhone, whose flood often overflows its banks, overwhelming everything. Between the towns of Sion and St. Maurice the valley bends in the shape of an elbow, and below St. Maurice it is so narrow that it hardly allows room for more than the river itself and a narrow road. An old tower stands here on the mountain side, as a sentry to mark the boundary of the canton of Vallais, opposite the stone bridge by the toll-house; and here begins the canton Vaud, not far from the town of Bex. As you advance you notice the increase of fertility, you seem to have come into a garden of chestnuts and walnut-trees; here and there are cypresses and pomegranates in flower; there is a southern warmth, as if you had come into Italy.

Rudy arrived at Bex, finished his business, and looked about him; but never a lad from the mill, not to mention Babette, could he see. This was not what he wished.

It was now towards evening; the air was full of the scent of the wild thyme and of the flowers of the limes; a shining veil seemed to hang over the wooded mountains, with a stillness, not of sleep, nor of

17

death, but rather as if nature were holding its breath, in order to have its likeness photographed on the blue vault of heaven. Here and there between the trees, and across the green fields stood poles, to support the telegraph wires already carried through that tranquil valley; by one of these leaned an object, so still that it might have been mistaken for a tree-stump, but it was Rudy, who was as still and quiet as everything about him; he was not asleep, and he certainly was not dead. But thoughts were rushing through his brain, thoughts mighty and overwhelming, which were to mold his future.

His eyes were directed to one point amidst the leaves, one light in the miller's parlor where Babette lived. So still was Rudy standing, that you might believe he was taking aim at a chamois, for the chamois will sometimes stand for an instant as if a part of the rock, and then suddenly, startled by the rolling of a stone, will spring away; and so it was with Rudy—a sudden thought startled him.

"Never give up!" he cried. "Call at the mill! Good evening to the miller, good day to Babette. A man doesn't fall when he doesn't think about it; Babette must see me at some time if I am ever to be her husband."

Rudy laughed, for he was of good cheer, and he went to the mill; he knew well enough what he wished for—he wished for Babette.

The river, with its yellowish water, rushed along, and the willows and limes overhung its banks; Rudy went up the path, and as it says in the old children's song:

"to the miller's house,
But found no one at home
Except little Puss!"

The parlor cat stood on the steps, put up his back, and said "Miou!" but Rudy had no thought for that speech; he knocked at the door; no one heard, no one opened it. "Miou!" said the cat. If Rudy had been little, he would have understood animals' language, and known that the cat said: "There's no one at home!" So he went over to the mill to ask, and there he got the information. The master had gone on a journey, as far as the town of Interlaken "*inter lacūs*, between the lakes," as the schoolmaster, Annette's father, had explained it in a lesson. The miller was far away, and Babette with him; there was a grand shooting competition — it began to-morrow, and went on for eight days. Switzers from all the German cantons would be there.

Unlucky Rudy, you might say, this was not a fortunate time to come to Bex; so he turned and marched above St. Maurice and Sion to his own valley and his own mountains; but he was not disheartened. The sun rose next morning, but his spirits were already high, for they had never set.

"Babette is at Interlaken, many days' journey from hence," he said to himself. "It is a long way there if one goes by the high road, but it is not so far if you strike across the mountains, as I have often done in chamois-hunting. There is my old home, where I lived when little with my grandfather; and the shooting-match is at Interlaken! I will be the best of them; and I will be with Babette, when I have made acquaintance with her."

With his light knapsack, containing his Sunday suit and his gun and game-bag, Rudy went up the mountain by the short way, which was, however, pretty long; but the shooting-match only began that day and was to last over a week, and all that time, he was told, the miller and Babette would spend with their relations at Interlaken. So Rudy crossed the Gemmi, meaning to come down near Grindelwald.

Healthy and joyful, he stepped along, up in the fresh, the light, the invigorating   mountain air. The valley sank deeper, the horizon opened wider; here was a snow-peak, and there another, and soon he could see the whole shining range of the Alps. Rudy knew every snow-mountain, and he made straight for the Schreckhorn, which raised its white-sprinkled, stony fingers high into the blue air.

At length he crossed the highest ridge. The pastures stretched down towards his own valley; the air was light, and he felt merry; mountain and valley smiled with abundance of flowers and verdure; his heart was full of thoughts of youth: one should never become old, one need never die; to live, to conquer, to be happy! free as a bird — and he felt like a bird. And the swallows flew by him, and sang, as they used to do in his childhood: "We and you, and you and we!" All was soaring and rejoicing.

Below lay the velvety green meadow, sprinkled with brown châlets, and the Lütschine humming and rushing. He saw the glacier, with its bottle-green edges covered with earth-soiled snow; he saw the deep fissures, and the upper and the lower glacier. The sound of the church bells came to him, as if they were ringing to welcome him home; his heart beat more strongly, and swelled so that Babette was forgotten for a moment, so large was his heart and so full of memories!

He again went along the way where he had stood as a little urchin with the other children, and sold the carved châlets. He saw among the pines his grandfather's house, but strangers now lived in it. Children came along the path to sell things, and one of them offered him an Alpine rose; Rudy took it as a good omen, and he thought of Babette. He soon crossed the bridge where the two Lütschine unite; the trees here grew thicker, and the walnuts gave a refreshing shade. He now saw the flag waving, the white cross on a red background, the flag of the Switzers and the Danes; and now he had reached Interlaken.

This, Rudy thought, was certainly a splendid town. It was a Swiss town in Sunday dress; not like other places, crowded with heavy stone houses, ponderous, strange, and stately. No! here it seemed as if the châlets had come down from the mountains into the green valley, close by the clear, rapid stream, and had arranged themselves in a row, a little in and out, to make a street. And the prettiest of all the streets — yes, that it certainly was! — had sprung up since Rudy was here, when he was little. It seemed to have been built of all the charming châlets which his grandfather had carved and stored in the cabinet at home, and they had grown up here by some power like the old, oldest chestnut-trees. Each house was a hotel, with carved woodwork on the windows and doors, and a projecting roof, and was elegantly built; and in front of the house was a flower-garden, between it and the broad, macadamized road; all the houses stood on one side of the road, so as not to hide the fresh green meadows, where the cows wandered about with bells like those in the high Alpine pastures. It seemed to be in the midst of lofty mountains, which had drawn apart in one direction to allow the snow-clad peak of the Jungfrau to be seen, most lovely of all the Swiss mountains.

There were a great many well-dressed visitors from foreign countries as well as many Switzers from the different cantons. Each competitor had his number in a garland on his hat. Singing and playing on all kinds of instruments were to be heard everywhere, mingled with cries and shouts. Mottoes were put up on the houses and bridges, flags and pennons floated in the breeze; the crack of the rifles was frequently heard, and Rudy thought this the sweetest sound of all; indeed, in the excitement of the moment he quite forgot Babette, although he had come on purpose to meet her.

The marksmen now went in the direction of the target. Rudy went with them, and was the best shot of them all — he hit the bull's-eye every time.

"Who is that young stranger who shoots so well?" the onlookers asked each other. "He talks French as they do in canton Vallais. But he also speaks German very well," others replied.

"They say he was brought up near Grindelwald," one of the competitors remarked.

There was life in the fellow, his eyes shone, his arm was steady, and for that reason he never failed in hitting the mark. Courage comes with success, but Rudy had a store of natural courage. Admiring friends soon gathered around him, and complimented him on his success; he altogether forgot Babette. Then some one laid his hand on his shoulder, and spoke to him in French.

"You belong to the canton of Vallais?"

Rudy turned, and saw a burly individual with a rosy, good-humored face. It was the wealthy miller from Bex; his stout form almost concealed the pretty, slim Babette, but she looked at Rudy with her sparkling, dark eyes. The miller was glad that a rifleman from his own canton should prove the best shot, and should have won universal applause. Rudy was certainly in luck, for although he had forgotten his principal object in coming, she had now come forward to him.

When neighbors meet one another at a distance from home they generally get to talking, and make each other's acquaintance. Because Rudy was a good shot he had become a leader at the rifle competition, just as much as the miller was at Bex, because of his wealth and his good business; so they clasped each other by the hand for the first time; Babette also offered her hand to Rudy who squeezed it, and looked at her so earnestly that she quite blushed.

The miller spoke of their long journey, and how many large towns they had come through; and it certainly seemed to have been a very long journey, as they had traveled by the steamboat, and also by rail and by post-chaise.

"I came the nearest way," said Rudy. "I walked over the mountains; no road is too high for a man to come over it."

"And break your neck," said the miller. "You look just the man to break his neck one day, you look so headstrong."

"A man doesn't fall if he doesn't think about it," replied Rudy.

The miller's relatives in Interlaken, with whom he and Babette were staying, asked Rudy to visit them, as he was from the same canton. This was a chance for Rudy; fortune favored him, as she always does favor those who endeavor to succeed by their own energy, and remember that "Providence gives us nuts, but we have to crack them for ourselves."

Rudy was welcomed by the miller's relatives as if he had belonged to the family, and they drank to the health of the best shot, and Babette clinked her glass with the others, and Rudy thanked them for the toast.

In the evening they went for a stroll on the road by the big hotels beneath the old walnut-trees, and there was such a throng, and the people pushed so that Rudy was able to offer his arm to Babette. He said he was glad to have met the people from Vaud. The cantons of Vaud and Vallais were very good neighbors. He seemed so thoroughly pleased that Babette could not resist the inclination to press his hand. They walked together just like old acquaintances, and she was very amusing. Rudy was delighted with her naive remarks on the peculiarities in the dress and behavior of the foreign ladies; and yet she did not wish to make fun of them, for she knew that many of them were amiable and worthy people—indeed, her own godmother was an English lady. She had been living in Bex eighteen years ago, when Babette was christened, and she had given her the valuable brooch she was now wearing. Her godmother had twice written to her, and Babette was now hoping to see her and her daughters in Interlaken.

"They were two old maids, almost thirty!" said Babette; but you must remember that she was only eighteen.

Her little tongue was never still for an instant, and all that Babette had to say was intensely interesting to Rudy; and he told her all about himself—that he had frequently been to Bex, and knew the mill well, and that he had often seen her, though he did not suppose she had ever noticed him; and how he had called at the mill, hoping to see her, and found that her father and she were away from home, a long way from home, indeed, but not so far that he could not get over the barrier which divided them.

He told her a great deal more than this. He told her that he was very fond of her, and that he had come here on purpose to see her, and not for the rifle competition.

Babette was very quiet when he told her this; she thought he set too high a value on her.

While they continued rambling, the sun set behind the mighty wall of rock; the Jungfrau stood out in all its beauty and magnificence, with the green of the tree-clad slopes on either side of it. All stood still to admire the gorgeous spectacle, and both Rudy and Babette were happy in watching it.

"There is no place more lovely than this!" said Babette.

"No, indeed!" exclaimed Rudy, and then he looked at Babette.

"I must go home to-morrow," he said, after a short silence.

"You must come to see us at Bex," Babette whispered to him; "my father will be pleased."

CHAPTER V.

THE RETURN HOME.

OH what a load Rudy had to carry home with him over the mountains the next day! He had won three silver cups, two rifles, and a silver coffee-pot; this would be of use to him when he began housekeeping. But that was not the heaviest thing; there was something heavier and stronger which he carried with him — or which carried him — on that return journey over the mountains. The weather was wild, dull, heavy, and wet; dense clouds covered the mountain tops like a thick veil, quite hiding the snowy peaks. From the valleys he heard the sound of the woodman's ax, and huge trunks of trees rolled down the steep mountain sides; they seemed only like small sticks, but they were big enough for masts. The Lütschine rushed along with its continual hum, the wind shrieked, and the clouds hurried across the sky. Then Rudy discovered that a young maid was walking at his side; he had not seen her until she was quite near. She also was about to climb over the mountain. The girl's eyes had a strange power; you could not help looking at them, and they were wonderful eyes, very clear, and deep — oh, so deep!

"Have you a sweetheart?" said Rudy, for that was all he could think of.

"No, I have not," laughingly replied the maiden; but she did not look as if she spoke the truth. "Don't go round all that way," she then said. "You must bear more to the left; that is the shortest way."

"Yes, and tumble down a crevasse!" said Rudy. "You're a fine one to be a guide if you don't know better than that!"

"I know the way," she replied, "and my thoughts have not gone astray. Yours are below, in the valley, but here, on high, you should be thinking of the Ice-Maiden; people say that she does not love men."

"I fear her not!" exclaimed Rudy. "She had to yield me up when I was a baby, and I am not going to yield myself up to her now that I am a man."

25

It grew darker, and the rain poured down; then came the snow, dazzling and bewildering.

"Take my hand," said the maiden, "I will help you;" and she touched him with her ice-cold fingers.

"You needn't help me!" returned Rudy; "I don't need a girl to teach me to climb!" and he hurried on, leaving her behind. The snow came down all around him, the wind shrieked, and he heard strange sounds of laughing and singing behind him. He believed she was one of the spirits in the Ice-Maiden's train, of whom he had heard tales when he spent the night up in the mountains as a boy.

The snow ceased to fall, and he was now above the clouds. He looked behind him, but saw nobody; yet he heard a strange singing and yodeling that he did not like, as it did not sound human.

When Rudy was quite at the highest ridge, from which the way tended downwards towards the Rhone valley, he saw above Chamonix, in a patch of blue sky, two bright stars shining and twinkling; they reminded him of Babette, and of his own good fortune, and the thought made him feel quite warm.

CHAPTER VI.

A VISIT TO THE MILL.

WHAT splendid things you have brought back with you!" cried his old foster-mother; and her eagle eyes sparkled, and her lean neck waved backwards and forwards more than ever. "You are lucky, Rudy! Let me kiss you, my dear boy!"

And Rudy submitted to be kissed; but he looked as if he regarded it as a thing which had to be put up with. "What a handsome fellow you are getting, Rudy!" said the old woman.

"Don't talk such nonsense," Rudy replied, laughing; but nevertheless he liked to hear it.

"I say it again," said the old woman. "You are very lucky!"

"Perhaps you may be right," he rejoined, for he was thinking of Babette.

He had never before been so anxious to go down the valley.

"They must have gone home," he said to
 himself. "They were to have been back two days ago. I must go to Bex."

So Rudy went to Bex, and found his friends at home at the mill. They received him kindly, and had brought a message for him from the family at Interlaken. Babette did not speak much; she was very quiet, but her eyes spoke volumes, and that satisfied Rudy. Even the miller, who had always led the conversation, and who had always had his remarks and jokes laughed at on account of his wealth, seemed to delight in hearing of all Rudy's adventures in his hunting; and Rudy described the difficulties and perils which the chamois-hunters have to face among the mountains — how they must cling to, or creep over, the narrow ledges of snow which are frozen on to the mountain sides, and make their way over the snow bridges which span deep chasms in the rocks. And Rudy's eyes sparkled as he was relating these hunting adventures, the intelligence and activity of the chamois, and the dangers of the tempest and the avalanche. He perceived as he went on that the miller grew increasingly interested

27

in his wild life, and that the old man paid especial attention to his account of the bearded vulture and the royal eagle.

Among other things, he happened to mention that, at no great distance, in the canton of Vallais, an eagle had built its nest most ingeniously under a steep projecting rock, and that the nest contained a young one which nobody could capture. Rudy said that an Englishman had offered him a handful of gold the other day if he could take him the eaglet alive; "but there is a limit to everything," said he. "That eaglet cannot be taken; it would be foolhardy to try."

But the wine assisted the flow of conversation; and Rudy thought the evening all too short, though he did not start on his return journey until past midnight, the first time he visited the mill.

Lights were still to be seen at the windows of the mill; and the parlor cat came out at an opening in the roof, and met the kitchen cat on the gutter.

"Have you heard the news at the mill?" said the parlor cat. "There's love-making going on in the house! The father doesn't know of it. Rudy and Babette have been treading on each other's paws all the evening under the table. They trod on me more than once, but I kept quiet, lest it should be noticed."

"I would have mewed," replied the kitchen cat.

"Kitchen behavior will not suit the parlor," said the parlor cat; "but I should like to know what the miller will say when he hears of the love-making."

What will the miller say, indeed? Rudy, also, wanted to know that; and he would not wait very long without finding it out. So a few days later, when the omnibus rolled over the Rhone bridge between Vallais and Vaud, Rudy was in it, in his usual high spirits, happy in the expectation of a favorable answer to the question he intended to ask that same evening.

In the evening, when the omnibus was returning Rudy was again inside; but the parlor cat had great news to tell.

"Do you know it, you from the kitchen? The miller knows everything. That was a fine end to the expedition! Rudy came here towards the evening, and he and Babette had much to whisper about; they stood in the passage which leads to the miller's room. I lay at their feet, but they had neither eyes nor thoughts for me. 'I am going straight in to your father!' said Rudy; 'that is the fair thing.' 'Shall I accompany you?' said Babette; 'it will encourage you.' 'I have sufficient courage!' said Rudy, 'but if you go too, he must look kindly on us, whether he will or no!' And they both went in. Rudy trod violently on my tail. Rudy is very clumsy! I mewed, but neither he nor Babette had ears to hear me. They opened the door, and they both went in, I in front; but I sprang up on the back of a chair, for I could not tell how Rudy would kick. But the miller kicked! and it was a good kick! out of the door, and into the mountains to the chamois! Rudy may aim at them, and not at our little Babette."

"But what did they talk about?" asked the kitchen cat.

"Talk? — — They talked of everything that people say when they go a-wooing: 'I am fond of her, and she is fond of me! and when there is milk in the pail for one, there is also milk in the pail for two!' 'But she sits too high for you!' said the miller; 'she sits on grits, on golden grits; you can't reach her!' 'Nothing sits so high that a man can't reach it, if he will!' said Rudy; for he was very pert. 'But you can't reach the eaglet—you said so yourself! Babette sits higher!' 'I will take them both!' said Rudy. 'Yes, I will give her to you, when you give me the eaglet alive!' said the miller, and laughed till the tears stood in his eyes; 'but now I thank you for your visits, Rudy; come again in the morning, and you will find no one at home! Farewell, Rudy!' And Babette also said farewell, as miserable as a little kitten that can't see its mother. 'An honest man's word is as good as his bond!' said Rudy. 'Don't cry, Babette; I shall bring the eaglet!' 'You will break your neck, I hope!' said the miller, 'and so put an end to your race!' I call *that* a kick! Now Rudy is off, and Babette sits and cries, but the miller sings German songs that he has learnt on his journey! I won't grieve over that now; it can't be helped!"

"But yet there is still some hope for him," said the kitchen cat.

CHAPTER VII.

THE EAGLE'S NEST.

FROM the mountain path sounds the yodeling, merry and strong, telling of good spirits and dauntless courage; it is Rudy — he is going to see his friend Vesinaud.

"You will help me! we will take Ragli with us. I must capture the eaglet up the face of the mountain!"

"Won't you take the spots of the moon first; that is as easy!" said Vesinaud. "You are in good spirits!"

"Yes, for I am thinking of getting married! But now, to be in earnest, I will tell you what I am intending!"

And soon Vesinaud and Ragli knew what Rudy wished.

"You are a daring lad!" said they. "You will not get there! You will break your neck!"

"A man does not fall down when he does not think of it!" said Rudy.

At midnight they set off with poles, ladders, and ropes; the way was through thickets and bushes, and over rolling stones, always up, up in the gloomy night. The water rushed below; the water murmured above, heavy clouds drove through the air. When the hunters reached the precipitous face of the mountain it was still darker, the rocky walls were almost met, and the sky could only be seen high up in a small cleft. Close by, under them, was the deep abyss with its rushing waters. All three sat quite still, waiting for daybreak, when the eagle would fly out; for they must first shoot it before they could think of taking the young one. Rudy sat down, as still as if he were a piece of the stone he sat on. He had his gun in his hand ready to shoot; his eyes were fixed on the topmost cleft, where, under a projecting ledge, the eagle's nest was concealed.

After waiting long, the hunters heard high above them a cracking, rushing sound; and suddenly they saw a great, hovering object. Two gun-barrels were pointed as the great black figure of the eagle flew out of its nest. One shot was heard; for a moment the bird moved its outstretched wings, and then slowly fell, as if with its greatness and the extension of its wings it would fill the whole of the chasm, and carry the hunters with it in its fall. The eagle sank into the depths; and brushing against the branches of trees and bushes, broke them as it fell.

And now the hunters began work. They tied three of the longest ladders together, setting them up from the last secure foothold at the side of the precipice. But the ladders did not quite reach; the nest was higher up, hidden safe below the projecting rock, where it was as smooth as a wall. After some deliberation they decided to tie two ladders together, and lower them into the cleft from above, and join them to the three which had been set up from below. With great trouble they drew up the two ladders and secured the rope; they were then suspended over the projecting rock, and hung swinging over the abyss, and Rudy took his place on the lowest rung. It was an ice-cold morning, and vapors rose from the black chasm. Rudy sat out there as a fly sits on a waving straw which some bird has taken to the top of some high factory-chimney; but the fly can fly away if the straw gets loose, while Rudy can only break his neck. The wind whispered about him, and below, in the abyss, rushed the hurrying water from the melting glacier, the Ice-Maiden's palace.

When Rudy began to climb, the ladders trembled and swung like a spider's web; but when he reached the fourth ladder he found it secure, for the lashing had been well done. The topmost ladder was flattened against the rock, yet it swung ominously with Rudy's weight. And now came the most dangerous part of the climb. But Rudy knew this, for the cat had taught him; he did not think about Giddiness, which hovered in the air behind him, and stretched its octopus-like arms towards him. Now he stood on the highest rung of the ladder, and found that after all it did not reach high enough for him to see into the nest; he could only reach up to it with his hands. He tested the firmness of the thick plaited boughs that supported the lower part of the nest, and when he found a thick and firm bough, he pulled himself up by it till he got his head and chest over the nest. But there poured upon him an overpowering smell of carrion; putrefying lambs, chamois, and birds lay here torn to pieces. Giddiness, which was not able to reach him, puffed the poisonous exhalation into his face, to confuse him, and below, in the

31

black gaping depth, over the hurrying water, sat the Ice-Maiden herself, with her long greenish hair, staring with deathly eyes like two gun-barrels, and saying to herself, "Now I shall capture you!"

In a corner of the nest he saw a large and powerful eaglet, which could not yet fly. Rudy fastened his eyes on it, held himself with all the force of one hand, and cast, with the other hand, a noose over the young bird. Thus, with its legs entangled in the line, it was captured alive. Rudy threw the noose with the bird in it over his shoulder, so that it hung a good way below him, and by the help of a rope he made himself fast till his toes reached the highest rung of the ladder.

"Hold fast! don't believe you will fall, and you won't fall!" this was his old lesson, and he stuck to it; he held fast, he scrambled, he was certain he should not fall, and he did not fall.

And now was heard a yodel, so vigorous and joyful. Rudy stood on the firm rock with his eaglet.

CHAPTER VIII.

"I HOLD FAST TO BABETTE."

"**HERE** is what you demanded!" said Rudy, entering the miller's house at Bex; and, setting on the floor a large basket, he took off the cloth, and there glared from it two yellow, black-rimmed eyes, so sparkling, so wild, that they seemed to burn and devour everything they saw; the short, strong beak gaped, ready to bite, the neck was red and downy.

"The eaglet!" shouted the miller. Babette gave one scream, and sprang aside, but she could not turn her eyes away from Rudy or the eaglet.

"You are not to be frightened!" said the miller.

"And you always keep your word!" said Rudy; "each has his own characteristic!"

"But how is it you did not break your neck?" inquired the miller.

"Because I held fast!" answered Rudy, "and that I do still! I hold fast to Babette!"

"First see that you have her!" said the miller with a laugh; and that was a good sign, Babette knew.

"Let us get the eaglet out of the basket; it looks dangerous. How it stares! How did you catch it?"

And Rudy had to tell them, and the miller stared, opening his eyes wider and wider.

"With your boldness and luck you can maintain three wives!" said the miller.

"Thank you! thank you!" cried Rudy.

"Yes; still you have not got Babette!" said the miller, and jestingly slapped the young hunter on the shoulder.

"Have you heard the news in the mill?" said the parlor cat to the kitchen cat. "Rudy has brought us the eaglet, and will take Babette in exchange. They have kissed each other and let father see it! That is as good as an engagement. The old man didn't kick; he drew in his claws, and took his nap after dinner, and let the two sit and wag their tails. They have so much to say, they won't be finished before Christmas."

Nor had they finished before Christmas. The wind scattered the brown leaves, the snow drifted in the valley and on the high mountains. The Ice-Maiden sat in her noble palace, which grows in the winter; the rocky walls were coated with ice, there were icicles ponderous as elephants where in the summer the mountain-torrent poured its watery deluge; ice-garlands of fantastic ice-crystals glittered on the snow-powdered fir-trees. The Ice-Maiden rode on the whistling wind across the deepest valleys. The snow carpet was spread quite down to Bex, and she could come there and see Rudy within doors, more than he was accustomed to, for he sat with Babette. The marriage was to take place towards the summer; he often had a ringing in his ears, so frequently did his friends talk of it. There was summer, glowing with the most beautiful Alpine roses, the merry, laughing Babette, beautiful as spring, the spring that makes all the birds sing of summer and of weddings.

"How can those two sit and hang over each other?" said the parlor cat. "I am now quite tired of their mewing!"

CHAPTER IX.

THE ICE-MAIDEN.

THE walnuts and chestnut-trees, all hung with the green garlands of spring, spread from the bridge at St. Maurice to the margin of the Lake of Geneva along the Rhone, which with violent speed rushes from its source under the green glacier — the ice palace, where the Ice-Maiden lives, whence she flies on the wind to the highest snow-field, and there, in the strong sunlight, stretches herself on her drifting bed. And as she sits there she looks with far-seeing glance into the deepest valleys, where men, like ants on a sunlit stone, busily move about.

"Powerful Spirits, as the Children of the Sun call you!" said the Ice-Maiden, "you are creeping things! with a rolling snowball both you and your houses and towns are crushed and effaced!" And she raised her proud head higher, and looked about her and deep down with deathly eyes. But from the valley was heard a rumbling, blasting of the rocks; menwere at work; roads and tunnels were being made for railways.

"They play like moles!" said she; "they are digging passages, therefore I hear sounds like musket-shots. When I move my castle the sound is louder than the rolling of thunder."

From the valley arose a smoke, which moved onward like a flickering veil; it was the flying plume from a locomotive, which was drawing a train on the recently opened railway, the winding serpent, whose joints are the carriages.

"They play at masters down below, the Powerful Spirits!" said the Ice-Maiden. "Yet the powers of nature are mightier!" and she laughed and sang, and the valleys resounded.

"Now there is an avalanche rolling!" said the men below.

But the Children of the Sun sang yet higher of human ideas, the powerful means which subdue the sea, remove mountains, fill up valleys; human ideas, they are the lords of the powers of nature. At the same moment there came over the snow-field, where the Ice-

Maiden sat, a party of mountain climbers; they had bound themselves to one another with cords for greater security on the smooth plain of ice, near the deep precipices.

"Creeping things!" said she. "You the lords of nature!" and she turned herself away from them and looked mockingly down into the deep valley, where the railway train was rushing past.

"There they sit, these *thinkers!* they sit in their power! I see them all! One sits proud as a king, alone! there they sit in a cluster! there half of them are asleep! and when the steam dragon stops they get out, and go their way. The thinkers go out into the world!" And she laughed.

"There is an avalanche rolling again!" said those down below in the valley.

"It will not reach us!" said two people behind the steam dragon; "two souls with one thought," as they say. It was Rudy and Babette; the miller also was with them.

"As luggage!" said he. "I am with them as something necessary!"

"There sit those two!" said the Ice-Maiden.

"Many chamois have I crushed, millions of Alpine roses have I snapped and broken, not leaving the roots! I will blot them out! Thinkers! Powerful Spirits!" And she laughed.

"There's an avalanche rolling again!" said those down below in the valley.

CHAPTER X.

THE GODMOTHER.

AT Montreux, one of the nearest towns which, with Clarens, Vernex, and Glion, form a garland at the northeastern end of the Lake of Geneva, lived Babette's godmother, an English lady of position, with her daughters and a young relative; they had recently arrived, but the miller had already paid them a visit, told them of Babette's engagement, and of Rudy and the eaglet, and of his visit to Interlaken — in short, the whole history — and they had been highly delighted and pleased with Rudy and Babette, and with the miller; and at last made them all three come, and so they came — Babette must see her godmother, the godmother see Babette.

Near the little town of Villeneuve, at the end of the Lake of Geneva, lay the steamboat which in its half-hour's journey to Vernex lies under Montreux. This is a shore which poets have praised; here, under the walnut-trees, on the deep blue-green lake, sat Byron, and wrote his melodious lines on the prisoner in the Castle of Chillon. Yonder, where Clarens is reflected with its weeping willows in the lake, wandered Rousseau, dreaming of Heloïse. The river Rhone glides forth under the high, snow-capped mountains of Savoy; here lies, not far from its outlet in the lake, a little island — indeed, it is so small that from the shore it seems to be a boat out there; it is a rock which, more than a hundred years ago, a lady had surrounded with a stone wall, covered with soil, and planted with three acacia-trees, which now overshadow the whole island. Babette was quite enraptured with the little spot — it was to her the most charming in the whole voyage; she thought they ought to stay there, for it was a most delightful place. But the steamboat passed by it, and stopped, as it always did, at Vernex.

The little company wandered hence between the white, sunlit walls which enclosed the vineyards about the little mountain town of Montreux, where fig-trees cast a shade in front of the peasants' cottages, and laurels and cypresses grow in the gardens. Half-way up stood the boarding-house where the godmother was living.

They were very cordially received. The godmother was a tall, kind lady with a round, smiling face; as a child she must have been like one of Raphael's angel heads, but now she was an old angel head, as her silvery hair was quite curly. The daughters were handsome, delicate-looking, tall and slim. The young cousin, who was with them, was entirely dressed in white from top to toe, with yellow hair and whiskers, of which he had so much that it might have been divided between three gentlemen, and he at once paid great attention to little Babette.

Handsomely bound books, pieces of music, and drawings were spread over the large table, the balcony doors stood open overlooking the beautiful, extensive lake, which was so bright and still that the mountains of Savoy, with the country towns, woods, and snowy tops, were all reflected in it.

Rudy, who was always bold, lively, and confident, felt himself out of his element, as they say; and he moved about as if he were walking on peas on a smooth floor. How slowly the hours passed! as if on the treadmill. And now they went for a walk, and it was just as tedious; Rudy might have taken two steps forward and then one back, and still kept pace with the others. They walked down to Chillon, the old gloomy castle on the rock, to see the instruments of torture, and death-chambers, the rusty chains on the rocky walls, the stony bed for those sentenced to death, the trap-doors through which the unfortunate beings were precipitated downwards and impaled on the iron spikes amidst the surf. They called it delightful to see all this. It was a place of execution, elevated by Byron's song into the world of poetry. Rudy felt it altogether the scene of executions; he leaned against the great stone window-frames and looked into that deep, bluish-green water, and over to the little solitary island with the three acacias; he wished himself there, and away from the whole chattering party; but Babette felt herself particularly cheerful. She said she had been unusually entertained; she found the cousin perfect.

"Yes, a perfect chatterbox!" said Rudy; and it was the first time that Rudy said anything which displeased her. The Englishman had presented her with a little book as a memento of Chillon; it was a French version of Byron's poem, *The Prisoner of Chillon*, which Babette could read.

"The book may be good enough," said Rudy, "but I don't care for the much-combed fellow who gave it you."

"He seemed to me like a meal-sack without any meal!" said the miller, laughing at his own wit. Rudy also laughed, and said that it was very well put.

CHAPTER XI.

THE COUSIN.

A few days later, when Rudy came to call at the mill, he found the young Englishman there. Babette was just offering him some boiled trout, which she herself must have garnished with parsley, it looked so dainty. That was quite unnecessary. What business had the Englishman here? What did he come for? To enjoy refreshments from the hands of Babette? Rudy was jealous, and that amused Babette; it gratified her to get a glimpse of all sides of his disposition, both strong and weak. Love was as yet but play to her, and she played with Rudy's whole heart; and though, as one may say, he was her happiness, the chief thought of her life, the best and grandest in the world; yes — but the more gloomy did he look, so much the more did her eyes laugh; she could almost have kissed the blond Englishman with the yellow whiskers, if by that means she could succeed in sending Rudy fuming away, for by that she would know how she was beloved by him. But this was not right or prudent of little Babette, only she was no more than nineteen. She did not think much of it; she thought still less how she could explain her conduct, which was more free and easy with the young Englishman than was suitable for the miller's modest and recently betrothed daughter.

The mill was situated where the highroad from Bex runs under the snow-covered peak which, the country people call the Diablerets, not far from a rapid, grayish-white mountain stream, like foaming soap-suds. This did not drive the mill; it was driven by a lesser stream, which was precipitated from the rock on the other side of the river, and was dammed up by a stone wall so as to increase its force and headway, and carried into a closed wooden basin by a broad channel away over the rapid river. This channel was so abundantly supplied with water that it overflowed, and made a wet, slippery path for those who used it as a short cut to the mill. The idea occurred to the young Englishman to use it, and dressed in white, like a working miller, he clambered over in the evening, guided by the light shining from Babette's room. But he had not learnt to climb, and nearly went head-foremost into the stream, but escaped with wet sleeves and bespattered trousers. Muddy and dirty he came below Babette's windows, clambered up into the old lime-tree and imitated the call of an owl, for he could not sing like any other bird. Babette heard it, and peeped through her thin curtains; but when she saw the white man, and easily guessed who it was, her little heart beat with fright and with resentment. She hastily put out her light, saw that all the window-bolts were fastened, and left him to hoot.

It would be terrible if Rudy were now in the mill, but Rudy was not in the mill; no, what was much worse, he was just below it. There was high talk, angry words; there would be fighting, perhaps murder.

Babette opened her window in alarm, called Rudy's name, and told him to go away.

"You will not let me stay!" he shouted; "then it is an appointment! You are expecting good friends, better than me! Shame on you, Babette!"

"You are detestable!" said Babette; "I hate you!" and now she was crying. "Go! go!"

"I have not deserved this treatment!" said he, and he went; his cheeks were like fire, his heart was like fire.

Babette flung herself on her bed, and wept.

"I love you so much, Rudy! and you can believe that of me!"

And she was angry, very angry, and that did her good, for otherwise she would have been deeply grieved; now she could fall asleep and sleep the invigorating sleep of youth.

CHAPTER XII.

THE POWERS OF EVIL.

RUDY left Bex, and took the homeward path up the mountains, in the fresh, cooling air, the domain of the Ice-Maiden. The thick foliage of the trees deep below him looked as if they were potato plants; the firs and the bushes appeared even less, the Alpine roses bloomed near the snow, which lay in separate patches as if it were linen put out to bleach. There was a single blue gentian, and he crushed it with the butt-end of his gun.

Higher up he saw two chamois. Rudy's eyes sparkled, his thoughts took a new flight; but he was not near enough to them for him to shoot with confidence; so he climbed higher, where only coarse grass grew among the blocks of stone; the chamois went placidly along the snow-fields. Rudy hurried on eagerly, surrounded by misty clouds, and on a sudden he stood in front of a precipitous rocky wall, and the rain began to fall in torrents.

He felt a parching thirst, his head was hot, but his limbs were cold. He seized his hunting-flask, but it was empty; he had not thought of it when he rushed up the mountain. He had never been ill, but now he had a presentiment of it; he was tired, he felt a desire to throw himself down and go to sleep, but everything was streaming with water. Strange objects vibrated before his eyes, but he saw on a sudden, what he had never seen there before, a newly-built low house, leaning against the rock, and at the door stood a young maiden. He thought it was the schoolmaster's Annette, whom he once had kissed at a dance, but it was not Annette, and yet he had seen her before, perhaps near Grindelwald, that night when he went home from the shooting match at Interlaken.

"Where do you come from?" he demanded.

"I am at home!" said she. "I am watching my flock."

"Your flock! Where do they graze? Here are only snow and rocks!"

"You are very clever!" said she with a laugh. "Here behind us, lower down, is a beautiful meadow! that is where my goats go. I take good care of them! I don't lose one; what is mine remains mine!"

"You are brave!" said Rudy.

"You also!" replied she.

"Have you any milk? Pray give me some, for I am intolerably thirsty!"

"I have something better than milk!" said she, "that you shall have! Yesterday some travelers came here with their guide; they forgot half a bottle of wine, such as you have never tasted; they will not fetch it, and I don't drink it, so you can have it."

And she came out with the wine, poured it into a wooden bowl, and gave it to Rudy.

"That is good!" said he. "I have never tasted any wine so warming and fiery!" and his eyes sparkled, and there came an animation, a glow into him, as if all sorrow and depression had evaporated; and the gushing, fresh human nature coursed through his veins.

"But this is surely the schoolmaster's Annette!" he exclaimed. "Give me a kiss!"

"Then give me the pretty ring you have on your finger!"

"My engagement ring?"

"Exactly so!" said the girl; and she poured wine into the bowl, and held it to his lips, and he drank it. The joy of living was in his blood, he felt as if all the world belonged to him, and why should he worry? Everything is for us to enjoy and to make us happy! The stream of life is a stream of joy; to ride on it, to let ourselves float on its surface, that is felicity! He looked at the young girl: it was Annette, and still it was not Annette; even less was it the goblin phantom, as he had called her, he met near Grindelwald. The girl here on the mountain was fresh as the new-fallen snow, blooming as an Alpine rose, and nimble as a kid, but still formed out of Adam's ribs, as human as Rudy. And he put his arms around her, and gazed

43

into her wonderfully clear eyes. It was only for a second, and in this—who can explain it? was it the spirit of life or of death that filled him?—was he raised on high, or did he sink down into the deep, murderous abyss of ice, deeper, ever deeper? He saw the walls of ice like blue-green glass; endless crevasses gaped around him, and water dripped sounding like chimes, and gleaming like pearls in bluish-white flames. The Ice-Maiden gave him a kiss, and it chilled him through his backbone and into his brain. He gave one cry of pain, dragged himself away, stumbled and fell, and it was night before his eyes. The powers of evil had played their game.

When he reopened his eyes the Alpine maiden was gone, as was also the sheltering cottage. Water drove down the bare rocky wall, the snow lay all round him; Rudy shivered with cold, he was soaked to the skin, and his ring was gone, his engagement ring which Babette had given him. His gun lay by him in the snow; he took it up and wished to discharge it, but it missed fire. Watery clouds lay like solid masses of snow in the crevasse; Giddiness sat there and lured on her helpless prey, and under her there was a sound in the deep crevasse as if a huge rock were falling, crushing and sweeping away everything that would stop it in its fall.

But in the mill Babette sat weeping. Rudy had not been near her for six days—he who was in the wrong, he who ought to ask her forgiveness, because she loved him with her whole heart.

CHAPTER XIII.

IN THE MILLER'S HOUSE.

WHAT horrid nonsense it is with these human beings!" said the parlor cat to the kitchen cat. "Now it is broken off again with Babette and Rudy. She is crying, and he does not think any more of her."

"I can't endure that," said the kitchen cat.

"No more can I," said the parlor cat, "but I won't grieve over it! Babette may now be the beloved of the red whiskers! but he has not been here since he wished to get on the roof."

The powers of evil have their game, both without us and within us. This Rudy had discovered and thought over. What was it that had taken place about him and in him on the top of the mountain? Was it a vision, or a feverish dream? Never before had he known fever or illness. He had made an examination of his own heart when he judged Babette. Could he confess to Babette the thoughts which assailed him in the hour of temptation? He had lost her ring, and it was exactly in that loss that she had regained him. Would she confess to him? It seemed as if his heart would burst asunder when he thought of her; there arose within him so many memories; he seemed really to see her, laughing like a merry child. Many an affectionate word she had spoken in the abundance of her heart came like a gleam of sunshine into his breast, and soon it was all sunshine therein for Babette.

She might be able to confess to him, and she ought to do so.

He went to the mill, and confessed, beginning with a kiss, and ending in the admission that he was the offender. It was a great offense in him that he could distrust Babette's fidelity; it was almost unpardonable! Such distrust, such impetuosity might bring them both to grief. Yes, indeed! and therefore Babette lectured him, and she was pleased with herself, and it suited her so well. But in one thing Rudy was right—godmother's relation was a chatterbox! She wished to burn the book which he had given her, and not have the least thing in her possession that could remind her of him.

"Now that's all over!" said the parlor cat. "Rudy is here again, they understand each other, and that is the greatest good fortune, they say."

"I heard in the night," said the kitchen cat, "the rats say the greatest good fortune is to eat tallow-candles and to have quite enough rancid bacon. Now, which shall I believe—rats, or a pair of lovers?"

"Neither of them!" said the parlor cat. "That is always safest."

The greatest good fortune for Rudy and Babette was close at hand; the wedding day—the most beautiful day, as they called it.

But the marriage was not to take place at the church at Bex, or in the miller's house; the godmother wished the wedding to be held at her house, and that they should be married in the pretty little church at Montreux. The miller stuck to it that this request should be complied with; he alone was aware what the godmother intended to give the bride for a wedding present, and considered they ought to make so slight a concession. The day was fixed. On the previous evening they were to journey to Villeneuve, and to proceed in the early morning to Montreux by boat, that the godmother's daughters might deck the bride.

"There will be a feast here the day after the wedding," said the parlor cat. "Otherwise I would not give one mew for the lot."

"There *will* be a feast!" said the kitchen cat; "ducks and pigeons are killed, and a whole deer hangs on the wall. It makes my mouth water to look at it! In the morning they start on their journey."

Yes, in the morning! This evening Rudy and Babette sat together, as betrothed, for the last time at the mill.

Out of doors was the Alpine glow, the evening bells chimed, the daughters of the sunbeams sang: "May the best thing happen!"

CHAPTER XIV.

VISIONS IN THE NIGHT.

THE sun was set, the clouds came down in the Rhone valley between the high mountains, the wind blew from the south, a wind from Africa, but, over the high Alps, a tempest, rending the clouds asunder, and, when the wind had swept by, for one instant it was quite still; the torn clouds hung in fantastic shapes among the tree-clad mountains, and over the rushing Rhone; they hung in shapes like antediluvian monsters, like eagles hovering in the air and like frogs leaping in a pool; they came down over the rapid stream, they sailed over it although they sailed in the air. The river bore on its surface a pine-tree torn up by the roots, watery eddies flowed before it; that was Giddiness—there were more than one—moving in a circle on the onward-rushing stream. The moon shone on the snow-covered mountain tops, on the black woods and the strange white clouds, visions of night, spirits of the powers of nature; the mountain peasants saw them through the windows, they sailed below in crowds before the Ice-Maiden who came from her glacier palace, and sat on her frail-craft, the uprooted pine-tree, carrying the glacier water with her down the stream to the open lake.

"The wedding guests are coming!" That was what whistled and sang in the air and the water.

There were visions without and visions within. Babette dreamed a strange dream.

It appeared to her as if she was married to Rudy, and that many years had passed. He was now hunting chamois, but she was at home, and there sat with her the young Englishman with the yellow whiskers. His glances were warm, his words had a power of witchcraft; he held out his hands to her, and she was obliged to follow him. They left her home and went down the mountain, ever down, and it seemed to Babette as if there lay a burden on her heart, which was always growing heavier. It was a sin against Rudy, a sin against God. And then on a sudden she was standing deserted; her clothes were torn by the thorns, her hair was gray. She looked up in her grief, and on the edge of a cliff she saw Rudy. She held out her arms towards him, but did not venture to call or pray. Nor would it have helped her, for she quickly saw that it was not he, but only his hunting-jacket and hat, which were hanging on his alpenstock, as hunters set them to deceive the chamois. And in the depth of her affliction Babette wailed out: "Oh, that I had died on the day I was married, the day of my greatest happiness! that would have been a happy life! that would have been the best thing that could happen for me and Rudy! None knows his future!" and in her impious grief she precipitated herself into a deep chasm in the rocks. The spell was broken, and with a cry she awoke.

The dream had vanished, but she knew that she had dreamed something dreadful, and that she had dreamed of the young Englishman, whom she had not seen or thought of for several months. Was he in Montreux? Was she about to see him at the wedding? Her pretty lips tightened at the thought, and she knit her brows. But soon there came a smile, and her eyes gleamed; the sun was shining so beautifully outside, and the morning was that of her wedding with Rudy.

He was already in the parlor when she came down, and soon they were away to Villeneuve. They were a very happy couple; and the miller with them laughed and beamed in the highest spirits; he was a good father and an upright man.

"Now we are the masters at home!" said the parlor cat.

CHAPTER XV.

CONCLUSION.

IT was not yet evening when the three happy people reached Villeneuve, and sat down to their repast. After dinner the miller sat in an easy-chair with his pipe, and took a little nap. The young couple went arm in arm out of the town, then by the carriage road under the rocks so thick with bushes, skirting the deep bluish-green lake. The gloomy Chillon reflected its gray walls and massive towers in the clear water; the little island with the three acacia trees lay still nearer, appearing like a bouquet in the lake.

"It must be delightful out there!" said Babette; she had still the strongest inclination to go there, and that wish could be immediately fulfilled; there lay a boat by the bank, the line that held it was easy to unfasten. They could not see any one from whom to ask permission, and so they took the boat, for Rudy could row well.

The oars caught hold of the water like the fins of a fish, the water that is so pliable and yet so strong, that is all a back to bear, all a mouth to devour, mildly smiling, softness itself, and yet overwhelming and strong to rend asunder. The water foamed in the wake of the boat, in which in a few minutes the couple had gained the island, where they landed. There was not more than room enough on it for two to dance.

Rudy turned Babette round two or three times, and then, hand in hand, they seated themselves on the little bench beneath the overhanging acacias, and gazed into each other's eyes, while all around them was illuminated in the splendor of the setting sun. The pine forests on the mountains put on a lilac hue like heather when in flower, and where the trees ceased and the bare rock came into view it glowed as if the mountain was transparent; the clouds in the heavens were lighted up as if with red fire, the whole lake was like a fresh, blushing rose-leaf. Already, as the shadows lifted themselves up to the snow-clad hills of Savoy, they became bluish, but the topmost peaks shone as if of red lava, and for one moment looked as if these glowing masses had raised themselves from the bowels of the earth and were not yet extinguished. That was an Alpine glow, such as Rudy and Babette could never hope to see the equal of. The snow-covered Dent du Midi had a splendor like the face of the full moon when it is rising.

"So much beauty! so much happiness!" they both said.

"The earth has no more to give me!" said Rudy. "An evening hour like this is a whole lifetime! How often have I felt my good fortune as I feel it now, and thought, 'If all were now ended, how fortunately I should have lived! How blessed is this world!' and the day ended; but a new one began again, and it seemed to me that it was fairer still! Heaven is infinitely good, Babette!"

"I am so happy!" said she.

"Earth has nothing more to give me!" exclaimed Rudy.

And the evening bells chimed from the mountains of Savoy, from the mountains of Switzerland; the dark blue Jura lifted itself towards the west in a golden luster.

"God give thee what is grandest and best!" exclaimed Babette.

"That He will!" said Rudy. "To-morrow I shall have it! to-morrow thou wilt be mine! my own little, charming wife!"

"The boat!" cried Babette at that moment.

The boat, which was to take them back, had broken loose and drifted from the island.

"I will fetch it!" said Rudy, throwing off his coat; and he pulled off his boots, sprang into the lake, and took rapid strokes towards the boat.

Cold and deep was the clear, bluish-green water from the mountain glacier. Rudy looked down below, only one single glance—and he thought he saw a golden ring rolling, and gleaming, and playing—he thought of his lost betrothal ring, and the ring became larger, and expanded into a sparkling circle, and in that shone the clear glacier; interminable deep crevasses yawned around him, and the dripping water sounded like a carillon of bells and gleamed with bluish flames; in an instant he saw what we have to tell in so many words. Young huntsmen and young maidens, men and women, once swallowed up in the crevasses of the glacier, stood here alive, with open eyes and smiling mouth, and deep under them came the sound of church bells from submerged towns; a congregation knelt under the church arches, pieces of ice formed the organ-pipes, mountain torrents played on it. The Ice-Maiden sat on the clear, transparent floor; she raised herself up towards Rudy, kissed his feet, and there ran a deadly coldness through his limbs, an electric shock — ice and fire! one does not know the difference at the first touch.

"Mine! mine!" sounded about him and in him. "I kissed thee when thou wast little! I kissed thee on the mouth! now I kiss thee on the toe and on the heel — thou art mine altogether!"

And he was lost in the clear blue water.

All was still; the church bells ceased to ring, the last notes died away with the splendor on the red clouds. "Mine thou art!" sounded again in the depths; "Mine thou art!" sounded in the heights, from the Infinite.

The icy kiss of Death overcame that which was corruptible; the prelude was over before the drama of life could begin, the discord resolved into harmony.

It is beautiful to fly from love to Love, from earth into the Heaven.

Do you call that a sad story?

Unfortunate Babette! It was a fearful time for her! the boat drifted farther and farther away. No one on shore knew that the bridal pair were on the little island. Night drew on; the clouds descended and it became dark. She stood there alone, despairing, weeping. A furious storm broke over her; lightning illuminated the mountains of Jura, Switzerland, and Savoy, and thunder rolled continuously. The lightning was almost as bright as the sun; one could see each single vine as at midday, and then immediately everything would be shrouded in the thickest darkness. The flashes formed knots, rings, zig-zags; they struck round about the lake, they shone from all sides, while the peals were increased by the echoes. On the land people drew the boats higher up the banks; every living thing sought shelter, and the rain poured down in torrents.

"Wherever are Rudy and Babette in this furious storm?" said the miller.

Babette sat with clasped hands, with her head in her lap speechless with grief.

"In that deep water!" she said within herself. "He is deep down, as under the glacier!"

And she remembered what Rudy had told her of his mother's death, of his own rescue, and how he had been brought up as one dead out of the crevasse in the glacier. "The Ice-Maiden has him again!"

And the lightning flashed as blinding as a ray of the sun on the white snow. Babette started; the lake lifted itself at that instant, like a shining glacier; the Ice-Maiden stood there, majestic, pale blue, shining, and at her feet lay Rudy's corpse. "Mine!" said she; and round about was again darkness and gloom, and rushing water.

"Cruel!" moaned Babette. "Why then should he die, when the happy day was come! O God! enlighten my understanding! shine into my heart! I cannot understand Thy ways, but I bow to Thy power and wisdom!"

And God shone into her heart. A flash of thought, a ray of light, her dream of last night, as if it were real, seemed to shine through her; she called to mind the words which she had spoken: she had wished for *the best thing* for herself and Rudy.

"Woe is me! was that the seed of sin in my heart? was my dream a future life, whose string must be snapped for my salvation? Miserable me!"

She sat wailing in the gloomy, dark night. In the deep stillness she thought that Rudy's words sounded again, the last he had uttered: "Earth has nothing more to give me!" They had been said in the abundance of happiness, they came back to her in the depth of her grief.

A couple of years have elapsed. The lake smiles, the banks smile; the vines put forth swelling grapes; steamboats with waving flags hurry past, pleasure-boats with both their sails set fly like white butterflies over the expanse of water; the railway above Chillon has been opened, and leads deep into the Rhone valley. At every station visitors get out, they come with their red guide-books and read to themselves what remarkable things they have to see. They visit Chillon, they see from thence in the lake the little island with the three acacias, and read in the book of a bridal pair who, in the year 1856, sailed thither one evening, of the bridegroom's death and: "next morning the bride's despairing cry was first heard on the shore."

But the guide-books make no mention of Babette's quiet life with her father, not in the mill — strangers live there — but in the pretty house near the railway station, where from the windows she often looks out in the afternoon over the chestnut trees to the snow mountains where Rudy used to disport himself; she sees in the evenings the Alpine glow, the Children of the Sun encamping above and repeating the song of the traveler whose mantle the whirlwind carried away; it took the covering, but not the man himself.

There is a rosy luster on the snow of the mountains, there is a rosy luster in every heart where the thought is: "God lets that which is best come to pass!" but that is not always revealed to us as it was to Babette in her dream.

THE FELLOW-TRAVELER.

POOR Johannes was sorely afflicted, for his father was ill, past all hope of recovery. Besides their two selves, not a soul was present in the little room. The lamp on the table was flickering, and it was late at night.

"You have been a good son, Johannes," said the sick father, "and God will, no doubt, help you on in the world." And he gazed at him with mild and thoughtful eyes, fetched a deep sigh, and then died — though he only looked as if he had gone to sleep. But Johannes wept; for now he had nobody in the wide world — neither father, mother, sister, nor brother. Poor Johannes! He knelt down beside the bed, kissed his dead father's hand, and shed many, many bitter tears! But at length his eyes closed, and he fell asleep against the hard bedpost.

He had then a strange dream. He thought the sun and moon came down to him, and he saw his father again in full health and freshness, and heard him laugh as he used to do when he was pleased. A pretty girl, with a gold crown on her long, shining hair, presented her hand to him; and his father said: "Look what a bride you have won. She is the loveliest maid upon earth." He then woke, and all these fine things vanished; his father lay dead and cold in his bed, and nobody was near them. Poor Johannes!

In the following week, the dead man was buried. The son followed close behind the coffin, for he was never again to behold the father who had loved him so dearly. He heard them fling the earth down upon the coffin, and still saw a little corner of it left; but, at the next shovelful, even that disappeared. Then he felt as though his heart would break, so afflicted was he. They sang a psalm round the grave, and it sounded so beautiful that it brought tears into Johannes' eyes. He wept, and felt relieved. The sun shone down gloriously on the green trees, just as if it meant to say: "You must not be so mournful, Johannes. Look how beautifully blue the sky is yonder! Your father is up above, and is begging of the All-merciful that you may thrive at all times!"

"I will always be good," said Johannes, "then I shall join my father in heaven; and what joy it will be to meet him again! How much I shall have to tell him, and how much he will have to teach me about the delights of heaven, just as he used to teach me here on earth. Oh, what joy that will be!"

He fancied it all so plainly that he smiled, while the tears still ran down his cheeks. The birds in the chestnut trees kept twittering, "Twit! twit!" They were gay, although they had been at the funeral; but they knew that the dead man was now in heaven, and had wings much larger and more beautiful than their own; and that he was happy, because he had been good here on earth: and, therefore, they were pleased. Johannes saw how they flew from the green trees out into the wide world, and then he wished to fly away also. But he first cut out a large wooden cross to place on his father's grave; and when he brought it thither in the evening, he found the grave decked with gravel and flowers. This had been done by strangers, who all esteemed the worthy man who had gone to his last home.

Early the next morning, Johannes packed up his little bundle, and put into his girdle his whole legacy, consisting of fifty dollars and a couple of silver shillings, with which he meant to wander forth into the world. But first of all he repaired to his father's grave in the churchyard, where he repeated the Lord's Prayer, and then said, "Farewell!"

Abroad in the fields through which he passed, all the flowers looked fresh and lovely in the warm sunshine. And they nodded in the wind, just as if they meant to say: "Welcome to the greenwood! Is it not delightful here?" But Johannes turned round to give a last look at the old church, in which he was christened as an infant, and where he used to go with his father every Sunday to hear the service, and to sing his psalm; and in so doing he perceived, in one of the upper loopholes of the church tower, the little goblin belonging to it, who stood with his little pointed, red cap on his head, shading his countenance with his arm, so that the sun might not stream into his eyes. Johannes nodded farewell to him; and the little goblin waved his red cap, laid his hand on his heart, and then kissed his hand to him, to show that he was kindly disposed towards him, and wished him a happy journey.

Johannes now thought of how many beautiful things he should see in the wide world, so large and so magnificent as it was; and he went on and on much further than he had ever been before. He did not know the places through which he passed, nor the people whom he met. He was now abroad in a foreign land.

The first night he was obliged to lie on a haycock in the open fields, for he had no other bed. But this he thought was so nice a bed that the king himself could not be better off. The field, and the haycock, with the blue sky above, certainly formed a very pretty bed-chamber. The green grass, dotted with little red and white flowers, was the carpet; the elder bushes and hedges of wild roses were the nosegays that decorated the room; and his washing-basin was the brook, with its clear, pure waters, where the reeds were nodding to bid him good night and good morning. The moon was a large lamp, high up in the blue ceiling, and one that could not set fire to the curtains. Johannes might sleep in peace, and he did so, nor did he wake till the sun rose, and all the little birds around were singing: "Good morrow! Good morrow! Are you not yet up?"

The bells were ringing for church, for it was Sunday. The people were going to hear the preacher, and Johannes followed them, sang a psalm, and heard the word of God. He felt just as if he were in his own parish church, in which he had been christened, and where he sang psalms with his father.

In the churchyard were several graves, some of which were overgrown with very high grass. And he thought how his father's grave would grow to look the same in the end, as he would not be there to weed it and deck it. So he fell to work and tore up the grass, and set up the wooden crosses that had fallen down, and replaced the wreaths that had been blown away by the wind, thinking all the time, "Perhaps some one is doing the same for my father's grave, as I am unable to take care of it."

Before the church door stood an aged beggar, leaning on a crutch. Johannes gave him his silver shillings, and then went forth on his way, lighter and happier than he had felt before.

Towards evening there arose a violent storm, which made him hasten to find a shelter. Darkness soon came on; but at length he reached a small and lonely church that stood on a little hill.

56

"I will sit down in a corner," said he, as he went in; "I am so tired that I need rest." He then sat down, and folded his hands, and said his evening prayer; and before he perceived it, he was fast asleep, and dreaming, while a thunderstorm was raging abroad.

When he awoke, it was in the middle of the night, but the fearful storm was over, and the moon shone in through the window to greet him. In the middle of the church stood an open coffin, in which lay the body of a man, that was awaiting burial. Johannes was not fearful, for he had a good conscience; and, besides, he knew that the dead never injure any one. It is only living, wicked men that do any harm. Two such bad characters stood beside the dead man that was lying in the church awaiting burial, and they wanted to vent their spite, by not letting him rest in his coffin, and casting his poor body outside the church door.

"Why do you want to do so?" asked Johannes. "It would be very wicked. In Christ's name, let him rest in peace!"

"Oh, stuff and nonsense!" said the two hideous men; "he has taken us in. He owed us money, and couldn't pay it; and now he is dead into the bargain, and we shan't recover a penny! Therefore we will take our revenge, and he shall lie outside the church door like a dog."

"I have nothing in the world but fifty dollars," said Johannes, "which form my whole patrimony; yet will I willingly give them to you, provided you promise truly to leave the dead man in peace. I shall manage without the money. I have strong and healthy limbs, and a merciful God will assist me in times of need!"

"Of course," said the ugly men, "if you pay his debt, we will neither of us lay a finger upon him—that you may depend upon." And hereupon they took the money which he gave them, laughed aloud at his simple good nature, and went their ways. Then he laid the body carefully back into the coffin, folded the dead man's hands, took leave of him and continued his way through a large forest, in a contented frame of mind.

All around him, wherever the moon shone through the trees, he saw numbers of elegant little elves at play. His presence did not disturb them, for they knew him to be a good and harmless son of the earth; for it is only bad people who are not privileged to see the elves. Some of them were not taller than the breadth of one's finger, and wore their long yellow hair fastened up with gold combs. They were rocking themselves, two by two, on the large dewdrops that sparkled on the leaves and the tall grass. Now and then the drop would roll away, and down they fell between the long blades, occasioning a deal of laughter and merriment amongst the tiny folk. It was a pretty sight. Then they sang, and Johannes recognized distinctly all the pretty songs he had learned as a little boy. Large speckled spiders, with silver crowns upon their heads, were set to build suspension bridges and palaces from one hedge to another, which, when spangled by the dew, glittered like glass in the moonshine. These frolics continued till sunrise, when the little elves crept into the flower-buds and the wind took possession of their bridges and palaces, which were tossed upon the air as cobwebs.

Johannes had just left the forest, when the full-toned voice of a man cried out to him, "Ho there, comrade! whither are you going?"

"Into the wide world," said he. "I have neither father nor mother, and am a poor boy; but the Lord will help me in time of need."

"I am likewise going into the wide world," said the stranger. "Shall we keep each other company?"

"Willingly," said he; and so they walked on together. They soon felt a mutual liking for each other, for both were good; only Johannes soon found out that the stranger was much wiser than himself. He had traveled throughout nearly the whole world, and could tell of everything that existed.

The sun was already high when they sat down under a tree to eat their breakfast, just as an old woman was coming up to them. She was very aged, and almost bent double, and supported herself on a crutch-stick, while she carried on her back a bundle of firewood, which she had gathered in the forest. Her apron was tucked up, and Johannes saw three large rods of fern and willow twigs peeping out at each end. When she was quite close to our travelers, her foot slipped, and she fell with a loud scream, for she had broken her leg—poor old woman!

Johannes at once proposed that they should carry the old woman home; but the stranger opened his knapsack, and took out a box, saying that he had an ointment which would immediately make her leg whole again, and so strong that she would be able to walk home by herself, just as if the accident had never happened: only he required that she should give him in return the three rods she carried in her apron.

"That would be well paid," said the old woman, nodding her head in a peculiar manner. She did not like giving up the rods; but, on the other hand, it was still more disagreeable to be lying there with a broken limb. So she gave him the rods, and the moment he had rubbed her leg with the ointment the old dame got up, and walked much better than before. Such were the effects of the ointment; and truly it was not of a sort to be purchased at the apothecary's.

"What do you want with these rods?" asked Johannes of his fellow-traveler.

"They are three very pretty herb-brooms," said he, "and I like them, because I am a foolish fellow."

They then went on a good deal further.

"Look how overcast the sky appears!" said Johannes, pointing before them. "Those are frightfully heavy clouds."

"No," said his fellow-traveler, "they are not clouds; they are mountains—fine, large mountains—at the top of which one may overlook the clouds, and breathe fresh air. And delightful it is, believe me, to stand there! To-morrow we shall assuredly be far out in the wide world."

But they were not so near as they looked, and it took a full day before they had reached the mountains, where the black forests were towering up to the sky, and where blocks of stone might be found as huge as a large town. It seemed a somewhat difficult undertaking to cross them; therefore, Johannes and his fellow-traveler turned into an inn, in order to rest and gather strength for the next day's excursion.

A number of persons were assembled in the tap-room of the inn, where a man was exhibiting a puppet-show. He had just set up his little theater, and the people were sitting round to see the play. But, right in front, a stout butcher had sat himself down in the very best place, while a great bulldog by his side — who looked wondrously snappish — sat staring like the rest of the audience.

The play now began. It was a very pretty piece, with a king and queen, who sat on a splendid throne, with gold crowns on their heads and long trains to their robes; for their means allowed them to indulge in such luxuries. The prettiest little puppets, with glass eyes and large mustaches, stood at all the doors, and opened and shut them, to let in fresh air. It was a very agreeable play, and not at all mournful. But, just as the queen got up, and passed across the stage, no one knows what the huge bulldog took into his head; but, being no longer held by the butcher, he jumped right into the theater, and seized the queen by the middle of her slender waist, so that it cracked again. It was quite shocking to hear.

The poor man who exhibited the show was both frightened and sorry for the loss of his queen, for she was the most elegant puppet in his stock, and the ugly bulldog had bitten her head off. But when the rest of the spectators had retired, the stranger who traveled with Johannes said that he would set her to rights, and taking out his box, he smeared the puppet with the same ointment that had cured the old woman's broken leg. The moment this was done, the puppet was whole again, and could even move all her limbs of herself, and no longer required to be pulled by wires. The puppet was like a human being, except that it could not speak. The showman was vastly delighted, for now he had no longer any occasion to hold this puppet, who could dance of her own accord, which none of the others could do.

Late at night, when all the folks at the inn had gone to bed, somebody was heard to sigh so dreadfully deep, and so frequently, that the whole household got up, to see what could be the matter. The showman went to his little theater, for it was from thence the sighing proceeded. All the wooden puppets were lying in a heap; the king and his body-guard it was who were sighing so piteously, and staring with their glass eyes, because they wished to be smeared a little like the queen, in order that they might move of themselves. The queen knelt down and lifted up her pretty crown, saying, "Take this, but do smear my husband and my courtiers." The poor showman could not then help crying, for he was really sorry for his puppets. He immediately promised Johannes' fellow-traveler all the money he might earn on the following evening through his puppet-show, if he would only smear four or five of his prettiest puppets. But the fellow-traveler said he did not require anything but the large sword that he wore at his side, on receiving which, he besmeared six puppets, that immediately danced so gracefully that all living girls that beheld them were irresistibly impelled to dance likewise. The coachman and the cook began dancing, then the waiters and the chambermaids, and all the strangers present, as well as the shovel and the tongs — only the latter fell down at the very first leap. They had indeed, a merry night of it!

Next morning, Johannes started with his fellow-traveler, before any of the others were astir, and crossed the large forest of fir-trees, in their way up the high mountains. They climbed to such a height that the church steeples below looked like little blue berries in the green grass, and they could see for miles and miles around, where they had never yet been. Johannes had never before seen so much at once of the beauties of this lovely world. And then the sun shone so warmly through the fresh blue air, and the huntsmen's horns echoed so beautifully between the mountains, that tears came into his eyes, and he could not forbear exclaiming, "All-merciful God! what a kind Father Thou art to us, to have given us all the fine things to be seen in the world!"

His fellow-traveler likewise stood with folded hands, and gazed upon the forest, and the towns that lay in the bright sunshine. At the same moment, they heard a lovely sound above their heads, and on looking up, they perceived a large white swan hovering in the air, and singing as no bird had ever sung before. But its voice grew weaker and weaker, till its head drooped, and it slowly dropped down to their feet, where the poor bird lay quite dead.

"Two such beautiful wings," said the fellow-traveler, "so white and so large as this bird's, are worth some money; so I will take them with me. You see it was well that I obtained a sword." And he cut off the two wings of the dead swan at a single blow, and kept them.

They now traveled many miles across the mountains till they at length reached a large city containing hundreds of towers, that shone like silver in the sunshine. In the midst of the town stood a handsome marble palace, roofed with pure red gold, in which dwelt the king.

Johannes and his fellow-traveler did not care to enter the town immediately, but went into an inn, situated in the outskirts, in order to dress themselves; for they wished to look tidy when they walked through the streets. The landlord informed them how good a man the king was, and that he never injured anybody; but as to his daughter—heaven defend us!—she was a bad princess indeed! Beauty she possessed in abundance: nobody was prettier or more elegant than herself. But what of that? She was a wicked witch, and was the cause of many accomplished princes having lost their lives. She had given leave to everybody to woo her. Any one might present himself, be he a prince or a beggar; it was all the same to her. Only he must guess three things that she had thought of and questioned him about. If he succeeded, he was to marry her, and become king over all the land at her father's death; but if he could not guess the three things, he was then to be hung, or to have his head struck off. Her father the old king, was deeply concerned at all this: but he could not forbid her being so wicked because he had once declared that he would never meddle with her lovers and that she might do as she liked about them. Every time a prince came to try his luck at guessing, in order to obtain the princess's hand, he was sure to fail, and was, therefore, hung or beheaded. He had been warned betimes that it would be safer to desist from his suit. The old king was so afflicted at the mourning and wretchedness thus occasioned that, for one whole day in the year, he and all his soldiers used to kneel and pray that the princess might grow good; but she would not. The old women who tippled brandy used to color it quite black before they drank it; this was their way of mourning, and they could not well do more.

"What a shocking princess!" said Johannes. "She deserves the rod, and it would do her good. If I were the old king, she should have been thrashed long ago."

They now heard the mob cheering outside the inn. The princess was passing, and she was really so beautiful that everybody forgot how wicked she was, and therefore hurrahed. Twelve beautiful maidens, dressed in white silk clothes and holding golden tulips in their hands, rode by her side on coal-black horses. The princess herself was mounted on a snow-white steed, with diamond and ruby trappings. Her riding-dress was of gold brocade; and the whip she held in her hand looked like a sunbeam. The gold crown on her head resembled the little stars twinkling in the heavens, while her mantle consisted of thousands of splendid butterflies' wings stitched together. Yet, in spite of this magnificence, she was herself far more beautiful than her clothes.

When Johannes caught sight of her, his face grew as red as a drop of blood, and he was struck completely dumb; for the princess exactly resembled the beautiful girl with the golden crown, whom he had dreamed of the night his father died. He thought her most beautiful, and could not help loving her passionately. It could not be possible, thought he, that she was a wicked witch, who ordered people to be hung or beheaded when they were unable to guess what she asked. "But since every one, down to the poorest beggar, is free to woo her," said he, "I will repair to the palace, for I cannot resist doing so." Everybody advised him not to attempt such a thing, as he must inevitably fail like the rest. His fellow-traveler, likewise, warned him to desist; but Johannes thought he should succeed. He brushed his shoes and his coat, washed his hands and face, combed his pretty flaxen hair, and then went alone into the town, and proceeded to the palace.

"Come in," said the old king, when Johannes knocked at the door. Johannes opened it, and the old king came forward to meet him in his dressing-gown and embroidered slippers; he wore his crown on his head, and bore his scepter in one hand and his ball in the other. "Wait a bit," said he, putting the ball under his arm, to leave one hand free to present to Johannes. But the moment he heard he came as a suitor, he began to weep so violently that both ball and scepter fell on the floor, and he was fain to wipe his eyes with the skirts of his dressing-gown. Poor old king!

"Think not of it," said he, "you will fare as badly as all the others. Come, you shall see."

He then led him into the princess's pleasure-garden, and a frightful sight was there to behold! From every tree hung three or four kings' sons who had wooed the princess, but had been unable to guess her riddles. At every breeze that blew, all these skeletons rattled till the little birds were frightened, and never dared to come into the garden. All the flowers were propped with human bones; and human skulls might be seen grinning in flowerpots. It was an odd garden for a princess.

"Now, you see," said the old king, "your fate will be just the same as that of all the others whose remains you behold. Therefore give up the attempt. You really make me quite unhappy, for I take it so to heart."

Johannes kissed the good old king's hand, and assured him that all would be well; for he was quite enchanted with the lovely princess.

As the princess then rode into the palaceyard, accompanied by all her ladies, they went out to greet her. She was marvelously fair to look upon, as she presented her hand to Johannes. And he thought a great deal more of her than he did before; and felt certain she could not be a wicked witch, as everybody said she was. They then went into a room where little pages handed them sweetmeats and gingerbread-nuts. But the old king was so out of sorts, he could not eat at all. Besides, the gingerbread-nuts were too hard for him.

It was agreed that Johannes should return to the palace on the following morning, when the judges and the whole council would be assembled to see and hear how the guessing was carried on. If he succeeded, he was then to return twice more; but there never yet had been anybody who had been able to solve any question the first time, and in each case his life was forfeited.

Johannes felt no anxiety as to how he should fare. On the contrary, he was pleased, and thought only of the beautiful princess; and was quite confident that God would help him through his trials. Though how this was to be accomplished he knew not, and preferred not troubling himself to think about the matter. He capered along on the high-road, as he returned to the inn where his fellow-traveler was waiting his return.

Johannes could not cease expatiating on the gracious reception he had met with from the princess, and on her extreme beauty. He quite longed for the morrow, when he was to go to the palace and try his luck at guessing.

But his fellow-traveler shook his head mournfully. "I wish you so well!" said he. "We might have remained together a good deal longer, and now I must lose you! Poor, dear Johannes! I could weep, only I will not spoil your joy on the last evening that we may ever spend together. We will be merry—right merry! To-morrow, when you are gone, I shall be able to weep undisturbed."

All the inhabitants of the town had immediately heard that there was a new suitor for the princess's hand, and there prevailed universal consternation. The theater was closed; the pastry-cooks put crape round their sugar-husbands; and the king and the priests were on their knees in the church. This sadness was occasioned by the conviction that Johannes could not succeed better than all the other suitors had done.

Towards evening Johannes' fellow-traveler prepared a goodly bowl of punch, and said: "Now let us be merry, and drink the princess's health." But after drinking a couple of glasses, Johannes proved so sleepy, that he could not possibly keep his eyes open, and fell fast asleep. His fellow-traveler then lifted him gently out of his chair, and laid him in bed; and when it was quite dark, he took the two large wings he had cut off from the dead swan, and fastened them firmly to his own shoulders. He then put into his pocket the largest rod that he had obtained from the old woman who fell and broke her leg; and opening the window, he flew over the town, straight to the palace, where he placed himself in an upper corner of the building right under the princess's bed-chamber.

The whole town was perfectly quiet. The clock now struck a quarter to twelve, when the window opened, and the princess, wrapped in a flowing white mantle, and provided with a pair of black wings, flew over the city towards a large mountain. But the fellow-traveler made himself invisible; and as he flew behind the princess, he thrashed her with his rod till she bled. What a strange flight through the air it was! The wind caught her mantle, which swelled out on all sides like the large sail of a ship, and the moon shone through it.

"How it does hail, to be sure!" said the princess, at every blow she received from the rod; and such weather suited her. At last she reached the mountain, and knocked for admittance. Then came a noise like a clap of thunder, while the mountain opened, and the princess went in. The fellow-traveler followed her, for nobody could see him, as he was invisible. They went through a long, wide passage, where the walls shone brilliantly from the light of above a thousand glittering spiders that were running up and down and illuminating them like fire. They next entered a large hall built of silver and gold; red and blue flowers as large as sunflowers were beaming from the walls; but nobody could pluck them, for the stems were ugly, venomous serpents, and the flowers were the flames their jaws kept vomiting forth. The whole ceiling was covered with glow-worms and light-blue bats that were flapping their thin wings. It looked quite frightful. In the middle of the floor stood a throne that was supported by the skeletons of four horses, whose harness had been furnished by the red, fiery spiders. The throne itself was of milk-white glass, and the cushions were little black mice that kept biting each other's tails. Above it was a canopy of a deep-red cobweb, dotted with the prettiest little green flies that sparkled like precious stones. On the throne sat an old magician, with a crown on his ugly head and a scepter in his hand. He kissed the princess on her forehead, and placed her beside him on his splendid throne, and then the music struck up. Huge black grasshoppers played the jew's-harp, while the owl beat a tattoo on its own body, having no better drum. It was a ludicrous concert. Little dark-colored goblins, with a will-o'-the-wisp in their caps, danced about the room. But nobody could see the fellow-traveler, who had placed himself right behind the throne, where he could see and hear everything. The courtiers, who now came in, were very delicate and genteel. But anybody who could see what is what, would quickly perceive what they were made of. They were nothing better than broomsticks with cabbages for their heads, whom the magician had conjured into life, and whom he had tricked out in embroidered clothes. However, they did just as well, as they were only wanted for show.

After a little dancing, the princess related to the magician that she had a new suitor, and consulted him as to what she should ask him next morning when he came to the palace.

"I will tell you what," said the magician; "you must choose something easy, and then he'll never hit upon it. Think of one of your shoes. He'll never guess that. Then you will have him beheaded, and mind you don't forget to bring me his eyes to-morrow night."

The princess bowed, and said she would not forget to bring them. The magician then opened the mountain, and she flew back; but the fellow-traveler followed her, and struck her so smartly with the rod, that she sighed most deeply over such a hail-storm, and hastened all she could to reach her bed-chamber through the window. The fellow-traveler then returned to the inn, where Johannes was still asleep, took off his wings, and went to bed likewise, for he might well be tired.

Johannes woke at an early hour next morning. His fellow-traveler got up, and told him that he had had a strange dream that night about the princess and her shoe, and therefore urged him to ask whether it was not her shoe that the princess was thinking about? For this he had learned from the magician in the mountain.

"I may as well ask that as anything else," said Johannes. "Perhaps your dream may turn out to be the truth, for I trust in God to help me through. Still, I will take leave of you, because should I guess wrong, I shall never see you again."

They then embraced one another, and Johannes went into the town, and walked to the palace. The whole hall was filled with people. The judges sat in their armchairs, with their heads propped up by eider-down cushions, because they had so much to think about. The old king stood wiping his eyes with a white pocket-handkerchief. The princess now entered. She looked more beautiful than even the day before, and saluted the assembly with charming grace. But she extended her hand to Johannes, saying: "Good morning to you."

Johannes was now called upon to guess what she had thought of. Bless me! how kindly she did look at him! But no sooner had he pronounced the single word "shoe," than she turned as pale as chalk, and trembled all over. Still, this did not serve her much, since he had guessed correctly.

But, goodness! how pleased the old king was—he cut a caper that was quite pleasant to behold! And all present clapped their hands, to cheer both him and Johannes, who had been successful in this, his first ordeal.

The fellow-traveler was likewise much rejoiced on hearing how matters had turned out. But Johannes folded his hands and thanked his God, who he felt certain would help him through the two next times. On the following day, he was to make a second attempt at guessing.

The evening passed much the same as the foregoing one. When Johannes had gone to sleep, his fellow-traveler flew after the princess to the mountain, and thrashed her more violently than before, having taken two rods with him. Nobody saw him, and he heard all that was said. The princess was to think of her glove, and this he repeated to Johannes, as if it had been a dream.So that he was able to guess correctly, which occasioned great joy amongst the inmates of the palace. The whole court cut capers as they had seen the king do the first time. But the princess lay on the sofa, and would not speak a word. All now depended on whether Johannes could guess right the third time. If he succeeded, he was to marry the beautiful princess, and reign over the land at the old king's death. But if he guessed wrong, he was to forfeit his life, and the magician would have his beautiful blue eyes.

On the preceding evening, Johannes went to bed early, said his prayers, and then fell into a quiet sleep. But his fellow-traveler tied his wings to his back, and put his sword at his side, and taking the three rods with him, flew towards the palace.

It was as dark as pitch, and there was such a storm that the tiles were flying off from the roofs of the houses, and the trees in the garden, where hung the skeletons, bent like so many reeds beneath the wind. It lightened every moment, and the thunder rolled along as though it was a single clap that lasted through the whole night. The window now opened, and the princess flew out. She was as pale as death, but she laughed at the bad weather, and thought it was scarcely bad enough. And her white mantle fluttered in the wind like a large sail, while the fellow-traveler thrashed her with the three rods till her blood flowed, and she could scarcely fly any farther. She managed, however, to reach the mountain.

"This is a violent hail-storm," said she; "I was never out in such weather before."

"There may be too much of a good thing," observed the magician.

She now told him that Johannes had guessed aright the second time, and should he succeed again on the following morning, he would then have won, and she would never again be able to come to the mountain, or to practise magic arts as she had hitherto done; therefore was she quite out of spirits.

"He shall not be able to guess it," said the magician, "for I will find out something that he will never hit upon, unless he is a greater conjurer than myself. But now let's be merry!" And then he took both the princess's hands, and they danced about with all the little goblins, wearing will-o'-the-wisp lights, that were in the room. The red spiders jumped just as merrily up and down the walls; it looked as if the fiery flowers were emitting sparks. The owl beat the drum, the crickets whistled, and the black grasshoppers played on the jew's-harp. It was a frolicsome ball.

When they had danced enough the princess was obliged to go home, for fear of being missed in the palace. The magician said he would accompany her, that they might be together a little longer.

They then flew away through the bad weather, while the fellow-traveler broke his three rods across their shoulders. The magician had never been out in such a hail-storm before. Just on reaching the palace, and on bidding the princess farewell, he whispered, "Think of my head." But the fellow-traveler heard him, and just as the princess slipped in at her bedroom window, and the magician was about to turn round, he seized him by the long black beard, and cut off his ugly head at a single stroke from his sword, so that the magician had not even time to see him. He then threw the body into the sea, to serve as food for the fishes; but he merely dipped the head in the waters, and then tied it up in his silk handkerchief, and took it to the inn, and went to bed.

Next morning he gave the bundle to Johannes, bidding him not open it till the princess should ask him what she was thinking of.

There were so many spectators in the large hall of the palace, that they stood as thick as radishes tied in a bunch. The council sat on their armchairs with the soft cushions, and the old king was dressed in new clothes; his golden crown and scepter had been furbished up; and the whole scene looked very solemn. But the princess was pale as ashes, and wore a coal-black dress, as though she were attending a funeral. "What have I thought of?" asked she of Johannes. And he immediately opened the silk handkerchief, when he was himself quite startled on beholding the ugly magician's head. Everybody shuddered, for it was frightful to look at; but the princess sat like a statue, and could not speak a word. At length she rose and gave her hand to Johannes, for he had guessed aright. She looked neither to the right nor the left, but sighed out: "Now you are my master! Our wedding will be celebrated this evening."

"So much the better," said the old king, "that's just what I wish." All present cried "Hurrah!" The soldiers on parade struck up their music in the streets, the bells were set-a-ringing, the pastry-cooks took the black crape off their sugar-husbands, and rejoicings were held everywhere. Three oxen, stuffed with ducks and chickens, and roasted whole, were placed in the middle of the market-place, and every one was free to cut a slice; the fountains spouted the most delicious wine; and if one bought a penny cracknel at the baker's one received six large biscuits as a present—and the biscuits had raisins in them!

Towards night the whole town was illuminated, the soldiers fired cannons, and the boys let off pop-guns; and there was a deal of eating, and drinking, and crushing, and capering at the palace. All the fine gentlemen and the beautiful young ladies danced together, and one might hear them from afar singing the following song:—

"Here are many maidens fair,
Who twirl like any spinning-wheel,
And tread the floor as light as air;
Still round and round, sweet maiden, reel,
And dance away the mazes through,
Until the sole has left your shoe."

But the princess was still a witch, and could not endure Johannes. This struck his fellow-traveler, and therefore he gave Johannes three feathers out of the swan's wings, and a small phial containing only a few drops, and told him to place a large vat full of water in front of the princess's bed, and when the princess was about to get into bed, he must give her a slight push, so that she should fall into the water, into which he must dip her three times, having taken care first to shake in the feathers and the contents of the phial. The magic spell would then be broken, and she would love him tenderly.

Johannes did all that his fellow-traveler suggested. The princess shrieked aloud when he dipped her into the water, and struggled out of his hands under the form of a coal-black swan with fiery eyes. The second time she rose to the surface the swan had become white, all but a black ruff round its neck. Johannes prayed to God, and made the bird dive down a third time, when it was suddenly transformed to the most beautiful princess. She was far lovelier than before, and thanked him, with tears in her eyes, for having broken the spell that bound her.

On the following morning, the old king came with all his court, and the congratulations lasted till late in the day. Last of all came Johannes' fellow-traveler, with his stick in his hand, and his knapsack at his back. Johannes embraced him affectionately, and said that he must not go away, but stay with him, for he was the cause of all his happiness. But his fellow-traveler shook his head, and said in a mild and friendly voice: "No; my time is now up. I have but paid a debt. Do you remember the dead man whom his wicked creditors would fain have ill-used? You gave all you possessed that he might rest in peace in his grave. I am that dead man!"

And at the same moment he vanished.

The wedding rejoicings now lasted a full month. Johannes and the princess loved each other dearly, and the old king lived to see many a happy day, and dandled his little grand-children on his knee, and let them play with his scepter. And Johannes became king over the whole land.

THE OLD BACHELOR'S NIGHTCAP.

THERE is a street in Copenhagen oddly named Hysken Strâde, and one naturally asks what Hysken signifies, and why Hysken at all. Common report says it is a German word, but in justice to the German tongue this is not the case, since it would then have been Hauschen, of which Hysken is the Danish corruption, and it means "the street of tiny houses."

For many a year it consisted of nothing but wooden booths, such as may be seen to this day in the market-place; possibly they were a little larger. The window-panes were not of glass, but horn, for at that time glass was too expensive for general use. Remember, we are speaking of many years ago. Your great-grandfather would have called them "the olden times." Yes, several hundred years ago.

Trade in Copenhagen was entirely, or nearly so, in the hands of wealthy Bremen and Lübeck merchants, whose clerks (for they themselves stayed at home) lived in the Hysken Sträde, in the booths of this street of tiny houses, and sold beer and groceries. Delicious German beer it was too, and all kinds for sale—Bremen, Prussian, and Brunswick, and spices of every variety—saffron, aniseed, ginger and above all pepper. Indeed, this was the staple commodity—hence the German clerks in Denmark acquired the nickname Pepper-folk—and since they were bound not to marry whilst in that country, many grew old and gray in service, and, as they performed their own domestic services themselves they became crabbed old fellows with whimsical ideas. This being so, it became usual to dub all crotchety old bachelors "pepper-fogeys," an expression now naturalized into the German language. This must be borne in mind if you would understand what follows.

These pepper-fogeys used to be unmercifully ridiculed, and told to pull down a nightcap over their ears and toddle off to bed, and many are the doggerel verses in which the nightcap figures. Yes, fun was poked at the pepper-fogeys with their nightcaps, just because they were so little known. And why should not one wish for a nightcap? you may ask. Listen, and I will tell you.

Hauschen Street was in those days unpaved, and wayfarers stumbled along as if it were a little side-alley. So narrow indeed was it, and so huddled together the booths, that in summertime a sail would be stretched from side to side, and strong was the fragrance of saffron and ginger pervading the stalls, behind which there served for the most part old men. They were not, however, clothed, as in the portraits of our ancestors, with peruke, knee-breeches, elegant waistcoat and tunic of ample cut, as you might suppose.

No, these old pepper-fogeys were no dandies to be portrayed on canvas, though one could well wish to have a picture of one as he stood at the counter, or betook himself with leisurely gait to church on holy days. A broad-brimmed hat, high in the crown, in which maybe the younger among them would sport a feather, a woolen shirt beneath a wide flapping collar, a close-fitting jacket, a loose cloak worn over it, and the trousers tucked into the broadly-peaked shoes, for stockings had they none. At his belt a knife and fork, and a larger knife for self-defense—a necessary precaution in those days.

Such was the costume of old Anthony, one of the oldest of the pepper-fogeys, only in place of the broad-brimmed high-crowned hat he always wore a sort of bonnet, under which was a knitted skullcap, a veritable nightcap, which never left his head. One or other, for he had two, was always on his head day and night. He formed a perfect study for an artist, so lean and wizened was he, so wrinkled his brow, his fingers so skinny, his eyebrows so bushy. He was said to be a native of Bremen; but in truth, though his master was, old Anthony was born at Eisenach, hard by the Wartburg. He never told the others, but pondered over it the more.

The old fellows did not often come together. He stayed in his own room, a dim light penetrating the opaque window-panes. Seated on the bed, he chanted his evening psalm. Theirs was not a happy lot— strangers in a strange land, heeded by none, save to be brushed aside when in the way.

On black nights, when the rain was pelting down outside, it was far from cosy within. Not a lamp visible, save that which threw a light on a picture of the Virgin painted on the wall. Hark to the rain beating in torrents on the masonry of the castle-wharf! Such evenings were long and dreary without some task. To arrange and rearrange things in the house, to make paper bags, to polish scales, is not work for every day. One must find other things to do, as did old Anthony. He would darn his clothes, and patch up his boots. And when at last he went to bed, true to his habit, down he would draw his nightcap, but soon raised it to see the candle was quite extinguished. He would snuff out the wick between finger and thumb, pull down his nightcap, and turn over to sleep. But it occurred to him to see if the ashes on the little hearth in the corner were quite burnt out; if they were damped enough, lest a stray spark should kindle a fire, and do damage.

Up he would get again, creep down the ladder (for steps they could not be called), and finding not a spark in the ash-pan, would go back in peace. But before he was half in bed he would have a doubt whether the bolts and shutters of the shop were secured, and down once more went the tottering feet, his teeth a-chattering with the cold, for never such biting frost as in late winter. Then, pulling up the coverlet and drawing down his nightcap, he would dismiss all thoughts of business and the day's toil from his mind. But no happier than before—old memories would weave their fantastic shapes before his fancy, and a many thorn lay hidden in the garlands.

When one pricks one's finger tears brim to the eyelids, and oftentimes old Anthony shed hot and bitter tears, that glistened like pearls. The largest pearls would fall on the coverlet with so sad a sound that it seemed his heart's strings were breaking.

Brightly would they glisten and illumine pictures of his childhood, never fading memories.

As he dried his tears on the nightcap, the scenes would vanish, but not the source of his tears: that lay deep in his heart.

The scenes did not follow the natural sequence of life; the saddest and most joyful together, but the last had the deepest shadows.

The beech forests of Denmark are admitted by all to be fine, but fairer still to the eyes of old Anthony were those around the Wartburg. More majestic and lofty the aged trees around the baronial castle, where the foliage of creepers trailed over the stone buttresses. Sweeter there the perfume of apple-blossoms. Vividly did he call them to mind, and a shining tear rolled down his cheek, wherein he saw two children, a boy and a girl, at play. The boy, rosy-cheeked and curly-haired, with clear blue eyes, was himself, the little Anthony. The girl had brown eyes, dark hair, and a merry, bright expression. She was the Burgomaster's daughter, Molly. The children were playing with an apple, which they shook to hear the pips rattle inside. They shared the apple and ate it up, all but one pip, which the little girl proposed they should plant in the earth.

"Then you will see something you'd never think of," said she; "an apple tree will grow, but not all at once." So they busied themselves planting it in a flower-pot. He made a hole, and she laid the pip in, and both heaped on the earth.

"Mind," said she, "you don't dig up the pip to see if it has struck root. Indeed, you mustn't. I did so — only twice — because I knew no better, and the flowers withered." Anthony kept the flower-pot, and every day the winter through watched it, but nothing was to be seen but the black earth. Then came the spring and warm sunshine, and two little twigs peeped forth from the pot. "Oh, how lovely!" cried Anthony, "they are for Molly and me."

Soon came another shoot; whom could that represent? Then another and yet another, and every week it grew, till it became a big plant. All this was mirrored in a single tear. Brush it away as he might, the source dwelled deep in his bosom.

Not far from Eisenach is a ridge of rocky heights, treeless and bare, known as the Venusberg.

Here was the abode of Venus, goddess of heathen mythology, known also to every child round about as Lady Holle. She it was who lured the knightly Tannhäuser, the minstrel of the Wartburg, to her mountain.

Little Molly and Anthony would ofttimes stand at the foot of the mountain, and one day she asked him, "Do you dare knock and say, 'Lady Holle! Lady Holle! open the door. Tannhäuser is here'?" But Anthony was afraid, only his playmate ventured.

"Lady Holle! Lady Holle!" she cried, loud and clear, but the rest so low and indistinct that he believed that she did not utter it. She looked so winning and was of such high spirit. When they were at play with other children in the garden, Molly alone of them all would dare to kiss him, just because he was unwilling and resisted. "I dare kiss him," she would cry, and throw her arms round his neck, and the boy would submit to her embrace, for how charming, how saucy she was, to be sure!

Lady Holle, so people said, was beautiful, but her beauty was that of a wicked temptress. The noblest type of beauty was that of the devout Elizabeth, tutelary saint of the land, the pious lady whose gracious actions were known near and far. Her picture hangs in the chapel lit up by silver lamps, but she and Molly bore no resemblance to one another.

The apple tree they had planted grew year by year till it was so large it had to be planted anew in the open air, where the dew fell and the sun shed his warm rays; and it flourished and grew hardy, and could bear the wintry blast, blossoming in the springtide as if for very joy. In the autumn it bore two apples — one for Molly, one for Anthony. Rapidly grew the tree, and with it grew Molly, fresh as one of its blossoms; but not for long was Anthony fated to watch this fair flower.

All things here on earth are subject to change.

Molly's father left the old home and went afar. Nowadays, by the railroad, it takes but some few hours, but in those times over a day and night, to travel so far east as to Weimar.

Both Molly and Anthony cried, and she told him he was more to her than all the fine folk in Weimar could be.

A year passed by — two, three years — and only two letters came: the first sent by a letter-carrier, the other by a traveler — a long and devious way by town and hamlet.

How often had he and Molly together read the story of Tristan and Isolde, and bethought them the name Tristan meant "conceived in tribulation." But with Anthony no such thought could be harbored as "She has forsaken me."

True, Isolde did *not* forsake Tristan; buried side by side in the little churchyard, the lime trees met and entwined over their graves. Anthony loved this story, sad though it was.

But no sad fate could await him and Molly, and blithely he sang as he rode in the clear moonlight towards Weimar to visit Molly.

He would fain come unexpected, and unexpected he came.

And welcome they made him. Wine-cups filled to the brim, distinguished company, a comfortable room, all these he found, but it was not as he had pictured it, dreamed of it.

Poor Anthony could not make it out, could not understand them, but we can. We know how one may be in the midst of others and yet be solitary; how one talks as fellow-voyagers in a post-chaise, boring one another, and each wishing the other far away.

One day Molly spoke to him. "I am straight-forward, I will tell you all. Since we were playmates together much has altered. It is not only an outward change in me, you see. Habit and will do not control our affections. I wish you well, Anthony, and would not have you bitter towards me when I am far away, but love, deep love, I cannot feel for you. Fare thee well!"

So Anthony bade her farewell. No tear bedimmed his eye, but he felt he had lost a friend. Within four and twenty hours he was back in Eisenach; the horse that bore him, bore him no more.

"What matter?" said he, "I am lost. I will destroy whatever reminds me of the Lady Holle. The apple tree—I will uproot it, shatter it. Never more shall it bloom and bear fruit."

But the tree was not injured. Anthony lay on his bed, stricken with fever. What can avail him. Suddenly a medicine, the bitterest medicine known to man, cured his fever, convulsing body and soul. Anthony's father was no longer the rich merchant he had been!

Troublous days, days of trial, awaited them. Misfortune fell upon the home; the father, dogged by fate, became poor. So Anthony had other things to think about than the resentment he cherished in his heart towards Molly. He must take his father's place, he must go out into the great world and earn his bread.

He reached Bremen: hardship and dreary days were his lot — days that harden the heart or sometimes make it very tender. How he had misjudged his fellow-men in his young days! He became resigned and cheerful. God's way is best, was his thought. How had it been if heaven had not turned her affection to another before this calamity? "Thanks be to heaven," he would say. "She was not to blame, and I have felt so bitter towards her."

Time passed on. Anthony's father died, and strangers occupied the old home. But he was destined to see it once more. His wealthy master sent him on business that brought him once more to Eisenach, his native town.

The old Wartburg was unchanged — the monk and nun hewn on its stones. The grand old trees set off the landscape as of old. Over the valley the Venusberg rose, a gray mass in the twilight. He longed to say, "Lady Holle! Lady Holle! open the door to me. Fain would I stay forever." It was a sinful thought, and he crossed himself. Old memories crowded to his mind as he gazed with tear-bedewed eyes at the town of childhood's days. The old homestead stood unchanged, but the garden was not the same. A roadway crossed one corner of it. The apple tree, which he had *not* destroyed, was no longer in the garden, but across the way.

Still, as of old, bathed in sunshine and dew, the old tree bore richly, and its boughs were laden with fruit. One of its branches was broken. Wilful hands had done this, for the tree now stood by the highway.

Passers-by plucked its blossoms, gathered its fruit, and broke its branches. Well might one say, as one says of men, "This was not its destiny as it lay in its cradle." So fair its prospects, that this should be the end! Neglected, forsaken, no longer tended, there between field and highway it stood — bare to the storm, shattered and rent. As the years roll by it puts forth fewer blossoms, less fruit — and its story comes to a close!

So mused Anthony many a lonely evening in his room in the wooden booth in a strange land, in the narrow street in Copenhagen, whither his rich master sent him bound by his vow not to marry.

Marriage, forsooth, for him! Ha, ha! he laughed a strange laugh.

The winter was early that year with sharp frost. Outside raged a blinding snowstorm, so that every one that could stayed indoors. And so it befell that his neighbors never saw that for two days his shop was unopened, nor Anthony been seen, for who would venture out if not compelled to?

Those were sad, dismal days in his room, where the panes were not of glass, and — at best but faintly lighted — it was often pitch dark. For two days did Anthony keep his bed; he lacked strength to rise. The bitter weather affected his old joints. Forgotten was the pepper-fogey; helpless he lay. Scarce could he reach the water-jug by the bedside, and the last drop was drunk. Not fever, not sickness, laid him low: it was old age.

It was perpetual night to him as he lay there.

A little spider spun a web over the bed, as if for a pall when he should close his eyes forever.

Long and very dreary was the time. Yet he shed no tears, nor did he suffer pain. His only thought was that the world and its turmoil were not for him; that he was away from them even as he had passed from the thoughts of others.

At one time he seemed to feel the pangs of hunger, to faint with thirst. Was no one coming? None could come. He thought of those who perished of thirst, thought how the saintly Elizabeth, the noble lady of Thüringen, visited the lowliest hovels, bearing hope to and succoring the sick. Her pious deeds inspired his thoughts; he remembered how she would console those in pain, bind up their wounds, and though her stern lord and master stormed with rage, bear sustenance to the starving. He called to mind the legend how her husband followed her as she bore a well-stocked basket to the poor, and confronting her demanded what lay within. How in her great dread she replied, "Flowers I have culled in the garden." How when he snatched aside the cloth to see whether her words were true, wine, bread, and all the basket held miraculously changed to roses.

Such was the picture of the saint; so his weary eyes imagined her standing by his bed in the little room in a strange land. He raised his head and gazed into her gentle eyes. All round seemed bright and rosy-hued. The flowers expanded, and now he smelt the perfume of apple-blossoms; he saw an apple tree in bloom, its branches waving above him. It was the tree the children had planted in the flower-pot together.

And the drooping leaves fanned his burning brow and cooled his parched lips; they were as wine and bread on his breast. He felt calm and serene, and composed himself to sleep.

"Now I will sleep, and it will bring relief. To-morrow I shall be well; to-morrow I will rise. I planted it in love; I see it now in heavenly radiance." And he sunk to rest.

On the morrow—the third day—the storm abated, and his neighbors came to see old Anthony. Prone he lay, clasping in death his old nightcap in his hands.

Where were the tears he had shed, where the pearls? They were still in the nightcap. True pearls change not. The old thoughts, the tears of long ago—yes, they remained in the nightcap of the old pepper-fogey.

Covet not the old nightcap. It would make your brow burn, your pulse beat fast. It brings strange dreams. The first to put it on was to know this. It was fifty years later that the Burgomaster, who lived in luxury with wife and children, put it on. His dreams were of unhappy love, ruin, and starvation.

"Phew! how the nightcap burns," said he, and tore it off, and pearl after pearl fell from it to the ground. "Good gracious!" cried the Burgomaster, "I must be feverish; how they sparkle before my eyes." They were tears, wept half a century before by old Anthony of Eisenach.

To all who thereafter put on the nightcap came agitating visions and dreams. His own history was changed to that of Anthony, till it became quite a story. There may be many such stories; we, however, leave others to tell them.

We have told the first, and our last words shall be, "Don't wish for the old bachelor's nightcap."

THE GARDEN OF PARADISE.

THE FOUR WINDS.

THERE once lived a king's son, who possessed a larger and more beautiful collection of books than anybody ever had before. He could read in their pages all the events that had ever taken place in the world, and see them illustrated by the most exquisite engravings. He could obtain information about any people or any country, only not a word could he ever find as to the geographical position of the Garden of the World; and this was just what he was most desirous of ascertaining.

His grandmother had told him, when he was quite a little boy, and beginning to go to school, that each flower in the Garden of the World was the most delicious cake, and had its stamina filled with luscious wine; on one stood written historical facts, on another geography or arithmetical tables — and so one need only eat cakes to learn one's lesson, and the more one ate, the more history, geography, and arithmetic one acquired.

He used to believe this. But when he grew a little older, and had learned more and become wiser, he began to understand that there must be better delights than these in the Garden of the World.

He was now seventeen, and nothing ran in his head but this garden.

One day he went to take a walk in the forest, all alone, as he best liked to be.

As evening came on, the sky grew overcast, and there came on such a shower, that it seemed as if the heavens had become one vast sluice that kept pouring down water; besides this, it was darker than it usually is, even at night, except at the bottom of the deepest well. At every step, he either slipped on the wet grass, or stumbled over some bare rock. Everything was dripping wet, and the poor prince had not a dry thread about him. He was obliged to climb over huge blocks of stone, where water was running down from the thick moss. He was near fainting away, when he heard a singular rushing noise, and perceived a large cavern, lighted up by a huge fire, piled up in the middle, and fit to roast a whole deer. And this, indeed, was being done. A very fine deer, with its branching horns, was placed on a spit, and slowly turned round between the felled trunks of two pine-trees. An elderly woman, as bony and masculine as though she were a man in female attire, sat by the fire, and kept throwing in one log of wood after another.

"Come nearer," said she, "and sit by the fire, and dry your clothes."

"There is a great draught here," observed the prince, sitting down on the ground.

"It will be much worse when my sons come home," returned the woman. "You are in the Cavern of the Winds. My sons are the Four Winds of Heaven — can you understand that?"

"Where are your sons?" asked the prince.

"It is difficult to answer a silly question," said the woman. "My sons are now at it, with their own hands. They are playing at shuttle-cock with the clouds, up there in the King's hall." And she pointed above.

"Oh, that's it!" quoth the prince. "But you seem to speak rather harshly, and are not as gentle as the women I am accustomed to see."

"Because they have nothing else to do. But I must be harsh, to keep my boys in any order; which I manage to do, headstrong as they are. You see those four bags hanging on the wall? Well, they are every bit as much afraid of them as you used to be of the rod behind the looking-glass. I bend the boys in two, I can tell you, and then pop them into the bag, without their making the least resistance. There they stay, and don't dare come out till I think it proper they should. But here comes one of them."

It was the North Wind who came in, diffusing an icy coldness around. Large hailstones jumped about on the floor, and snowflakes were scattered in all directions. He wore a bearskin jacket and clothes; his cap of sea-dog's skin came down over his ears; long icicles clung to his beard, and one hailstone after another fell from the collar of his jacket.

"Don't go too near the fire at once," said the prince, "or your face and hands might easily get frozen."

"Frozen, quotha!" said the North Wind, with a loud laugh. "Why, cold is my greatest delight! But what kind of little snip are you? How did you come into the Cavern of the Winds?"

"He is my guest," said the old woman; "and if that does not satisfy you, why, you need only get into the bag. Do you understand me now?"

Well, this did the business at once; and the North Wind then began to relate whence he came, and where he had been staying for nearly a month past.

"I come from the Arctic Sea," said he, "and I have been on Bear's Island, with the Russian sea-cow hunters. I sat and slept at the helm, as they sailed away from the North Cape; but whenever I happened to wake, the petrels were flying about my legs. What comical birds they are! They will flap their wings suddenly, and then remain poised upon them, and quite motionless, as if they had had enough of flying."

"Don't be so diffuse," said the mother of the Winds. "And so you reached Bear's Island?"

"It's a beautiful place! There's a ballroom floor for you, as smooth as a plate! Heaps of half-thawed snow, slightly covered with moss, sharp stones, and skeletons of sea-cows and bears were lying about, together with the arms and legs of giants in a state of green decay. It looks as if the sun had never shone there. I blew slightly on the mist, that the hovels might be visible, and there appeared a hut, built from the remains of a ship that had been wrecked, and covered over with sea-cows' skins. The fleshy side was turned outwards, and it was both red and green. A living bear sat growling on the roof. I went to the shore, and looked after birds' nests, and saw the unfledged youngsters opening their beaks and screaming lustily; so I blew into their thousands of throats, and they learned to shut their mouths. A little farther on, the sea-cows were rolling about like giant worms with pigs' heads, and teeth a yard long."

"You tell your adventures right pleasantly, my son," said his mother; "it makes my mouth water to hear you."

"Then the hunting began. The harpoon was flung right into the sea-cow's chest, so that a smoking jet of blood spurted forth like water from a fountain, and besprinkled the ice. Then I thought of my part of the game. I began to blow, and set my vessels, the towering icebergs, to stick the boats fast. Oh! what a whistling and a bawling there was! Only I whistled louder than all of them. They were obliged to unpack the dead sea-cows, the chests, and the tackle upon the ice; I then shook snowflakes over them, and left them and their spoils to sail in their pent-up vessels towards the south, to drink salt-water. They will never return to Bear's Island."

"Then you have done mischief?" said the mother of the Winds.

"Let others tell of the good I may have done!" said he. "But here comes my brother from the West. I like him the best, because he smacks of the sea, and brings a nice bracing cold with him."

"Is that the little Zephyr?" asked the prince.

"Yes, that is the Zephyr!" said the old woman; "but he's not so very little either. Some years ago he was a pretty boy; but that is now over."

He looked like a wild man; but he wore a roller round his head, that he might not get hurt. In his hand he held a mahogany club, hewn from an American mahogany forest. It was no small weight to carry.

"Whence do you come?" asked the mother.

"From the wild forests," said he, "where tangled bindweed forms a hedge between each tree, where water-snakes lie in the damp grass, and where man seems to be a superfluous nonentity."

"What have you been doing there?"

"I looked into the deep river, and saw it had rushed down from the rocks, and then became dust, and flew towards the clouds to support the rainbow. I saw a wild buffalo swimming in the river, but he was carried away by the tide. He had joined a flock of wild ducks, who flew up into the air the moment the waters dashed downwards. The buffalo was obliged to be hurled into the precipice. This pleased me, and I raised a storm, so that the oldest trees sailed down the river, and were reduced to splinters."

"And was that all you did?" asked the old woman.

"I cut capers in the savannahs, I stroked wild horses and shook cocoanut trees. Oh! I have plenty of tales to tell! Only one must not tell all one knows, as you well know, good mammy." And he kissed his mother so roughly, that she had nearly fallen backwards. He was a shocking wild lad.

Now, in came the South Wind in a turban and Bedouin's flying mantle.

"It is very cold hereabouts!" said he, throwing wood upon the fire. "It is easy to perceive that the North Wind has preceded me."

"It is hot enough here to roast a northern bear!" said the North Wind.

"You are a bear yourself!" answered the South Wind.

"Have you a mind to be both put into the bag?" asked the old woman. "There! sit down on that stone, and tell us where you have been."

"In Africa, mother," returned he. "I was amongst the Hottentots, who were lion-hunting in Caffraria. The grass in their plains looks as green as an olive. An ostrich ran a race with me, but I beat him hollow. I reached the yellow sands of the desert, which look like the bottom of the sea. I met a caravan. They killed their last camel to obtain some water; but they only got a very little. The sun was scorching above, and the sand equally scorching beneath one's feet. The desert stretched out into boundless expanse. I then rolled in the fine loose sand, and made it whirl about in large columns. A fine dance I led it! You should have seen how dejected the dromedaries looked as they stood stock still, and how the merchants pulled their caftans over their heads. They threw themselves on the ground before me as they would before Allah, their God. They are now all buried beneath a pyramid of sand; and when I come to puff it away, the sun will bleach their bones, and travelers will see that others have been there before them: a fact which is seldom believed in the desert, short of some tangible proof."

"Then you have done nothing but mischief!" said his mother. "Into the bag with you!" And before he had time to perceive it, she had taken the South Wind round the waist, and popped him into the bag. He wiggled about on the ground; but she sat upon him, and then he was forced to lie still.

"Your sons are a set of lively boys!" said the prince.

"Yes," answered she; "and I know how to correct them. Here comes the fourth."

This was the East Wind, who was dressed like a Chinese.

"Oh! you come from that neighborhood, do you?" said his mother. "I thought you had been to the Garden of the World?"

"I am going there to-morrow," said the East Wind. "To-morrow will be a hundred years since I was there. I have just returned from China, where I danced round the porcelain tower till all the bells were set a-jingling. The government officers were being beaten in the street; the bamboo stick was broken across their shoulders; and these were people belonging to the several degrees from the first to the ninth. They cried out: 'Many thanks, my fatherly benefactor!' But the words did not come from their hearts, so I made the bells jingle, and sang! 'Tsing! tsang! tsu!'"

"You are a wanton boy!" said the old woman. "It is well you are going to-morrow to the Garden of the World, for that always improves your mind. Pray drink abundantly from the fountain of wisdom, and take a small phial and bring it home full for me."

"I will," said the East Wind. "But why have you put my brother from the South into the bag? Take him out again; I want him to tell me about the phœnix, for the princess in the Garden of the World always asks after him when I pay her my visit every hundredth year. Open the bag, there's a dear mammy, and I'll give you two pocketfuls of tea-leaves, all green and fresh, just as I plucked them from the bush on the spot where it grew."

"Well, for the sake of the tea, and because you are mammy's own boy, I will open the bag."

This she accordingly did, and out crept the South Wind, looking rather foolish, because the strange prince had witnessed his disgrace.

"There is a palm-tree leaf for the princess," said the South Wind. "The old phœnix, the only bird of his sort in the wide world, gave me this leaf. He has traced upon it with his beak the whole history of his life during the hundred years that form its span. She may, therefore, be now enabled to read how the phœnix set fire to his nest, and sat upon it as it was burning, like the widow of a Hindoo. How the dried twigs did crackle! and what a smoke there was! At length out burst the flames: the old phœnix was burnt to ashes, but an egg lay glowing hot in the fire. It burst with a loud report, and the young bird flew out; and now he is king over all the other birds, and the only phœnix in the world. He has bitten a hole in the leaf which I gave you, and that is his way of sending his duty to the princess."

"Now let us eat something," said the mother of the Winds. And they all sat down to partake of the roast deer. The prince sat beside the East Wind; therefore, they soon became good friends.

"And pray what kind of a princess may she be whom you are talking so much about and where lies the Garden of the World?"

"Ho, ho!" said the East Wind. "What! have you a mind to go there? Well, you can fly over with me to-morrow, though I must tell you no mortal ever visited it before. It is inhabited by a fairy queen, and, in it lies the Island of Happiness, a lovely spot where death never intrudes. Get upon my back to-morrow, and I'll take you with me; for I think it can be managed. But now don't speak any more, for I want to sleep."

And then to sleep they all went.

The prince awoke at an early hour next morning, and was not a little surprised on finding himself high above the clouds. He sat on the back of the East Wind, who was holding him faithfully; and they were so high in the air that forests, fields, rivers, and lakes lay beneath them like a painted map.

"Good morning!" said the East Wind. "You might just as well have slept a bit longer, for there is not much to be seen in the flat country beneath us, except you have a mind to count the churches. They look like chalk dots on the green board."

It was the fields and the meadows that he called the "green board."

"It was uncivil of me not to take leave of your mother and brothers," observed the prince.

"When one is asleep, one is to be excused," replied the East Wind.

And they began to fly quicker than ever. When they swept across the tree-tops, you might have heard a rustling in all their leaves and branches. On the sea and on the lakes, wherever they flew, the waves rose higher and the large ships dipped down into the water like swimming swans.

Towards evening, when it grew dark, the large towns looked beautiful. They were dotted here and there with lights, much after the fashion of a piece of paper that has burned till it is black, when one sees all the little sparks going out one after another. The prince clapped his hands with delight, but the East Wind begged him to let such demonstrations alone, and rather attend to holding fast, or else he might easily fall down and remain dangling on a church steeple.

Fast as the eagle flew through the black forests, the East Wind flew still faster. The Cossack was scouring the plains on his little horse, but the prince soon outstripped him.

"You can now see Himalaya," said the East Wind, "the highest mountain in Asia—and now we shall soon reach the Garden of the World." They then turned more southwards, and the air was soon perfumed with spices and flowers. Figs and pomegranates grew wild, and clusters of blue and red grapes hung from wild vines.

They now descended to the earth, and reclined on the soft grass, where the flowers seemed to nod to the wind as though they had said—"Welcome!"

"Are we now in the Garden of the World?" asked the prince.

"No, indeed!" replied the East Wind; "but we soon shall be. Do you see yon wall of rocks, and that broad cavern, where the vines hang down like a huge green curtain? That's the road through which we must pass. Wrap yourself in your mantle, for burning hot as the sun is just hereabout, it is as cold as ice a few steps farther. The bird who flies past the cavern feels one wing to be in the warm summer abroad while the other is in the depth of winter."

"So then this seems to be the way to the Garden of the World?" asked the prince.

They now entered the cavern. Oh, how icy cold it was! Only it did not last long. The East Wind spread out his wings, and they beamed like the brightest fire. But what a cavern it was, to be sure! The huge blocks of stone from which the water kept dripping down, hung over them in the oddest shapes, sometimes narrowing up till they were obliged to creep on all-fours, at other times widening into an expanse as lofty as though situated in the open air. It looked like a chapel for the dead, with petrified organs and dumb organ-pipes.

"We seem to be crossing through an abode of Death to reach the Garden of the World!" said the prince. But the East Wind did not answer a syllable, and merely pointed forwards where the loveliest blue light met their eyes. The blocks of stone above their heads rolled away into a mist that finished by assuming the shape of a white cloud on a moonlight night. They were now in a most delightfully mild atmosphere, as cool as the mountain breeze, and as perfumed as a valley of roses. A river, clear as the air itself, was running along, filled with gold and silver fishes; scarlet eels, that emitted blue sparks at every motion, were disporting in the depths of the waters; while the broad leaves of the water-lilies that lay on its surface showed all the tints of the rainbow; the flower itself was a reddish-yellow burning flame that received its nourishment from the water as oil feeds the flame of a lamp. A marble bridge, as delicately sculptured as though it had been made of lace and glass beads, led across the water to the Island of Happiness, where bloomed the Garden of the World.

The East Wind took the prince on his arm and carried him over. And the flowers and leaves sang the sweetest songs of his childhood, but in so lovely a strain of melody as no human voice ever yet sang.

Were they palm-trees or gigantic water-plants that grew on this favored spot? The prince could not tell, for never had he seen such large and luxuriant trees before. The most singular creepers, too, such as one only sees represented in gold and colors in the margins of illuminated old missals, or twined around the first letter in a chapter, were hanging in long festoons on all sides. It was a most curious mixture of birds, and flowers, and scrolls. Just by a flock of peacocks were standing on the grass displaying their gorgeous fan-like tails. The prince took them for live creatures, but found, on touching them, that they were only plants — large burdock leaves, which, in this favored spot, beamed with all the glorious colors of the peacock's tail. A lion and tiger were disporting with all the pliancy of cats amongst the green hedges, that were perfumed like the flower of the olive-tree; and both the lion and the tiger were tame. The wild wood-pigeon's plumage sparkled like the fairest pearl, and the bird flapped the lion's mane with its wings; while the antelope, usually so shy, stood near and nodded its head, as if willing to join them at play.

Now came the fairy of the garden. Her clothes were radiant as the sun, and her countenance was as serene as that of a happy mother rejoicing over her child. She was young and beautiful, and was followed by a train of lovely girls, each wearing a beaming star in her hair. The East Wind gave her the leaf sent by the phoenix, when her eyes sparkled with joy. She took the prince by the hand and led him into her palace, whose walls were of the hues of the most splendid tulip when it is turned towards the sun. The ceiling was a large radiant flower, and the more one looked at it, the deeper its calyx appeared to grow. The prince stepped to the window, and looked through one of the panes, on which was depicted Jacob's dream. The ladder seemed to reach to the real sky, and the angels seemed to be flapping their wings. The fairy smiled at his astonished look, and explained that time had engraved its events on each pane, but they were not merely lifeless images, for the leaves rustled, and the persons went and came as in a looking-glass. He then looked through other panes, where he saw depicted the events of ancient history. For all that had happened in the world lived and moved upon these panes; time only could have engraved so cunning a masterpiece.

The fairy then led him into a lofty, noble hall, with transparent walls. Here were a number of portraits, each of which seemed more beautiful than the other. There were millions of happy faces whose laughing and singing seemed to melt into one harmonious whole; those above were so small that they appeared less than the smallest rosebud when represented on paper by a mere dot. In the midst of the hall stood a large tree with luxuriant drooping branches. Golden, apples, both great and small, hung like china oranges amid the green leaves. From each leaf fell a sparkling red dewdrop, as if the tree were shedding tears of blood.

"We will now get into the boat," said the fairy, "and enjoy the coolness of the water. The boat rocks, but does not stir from the spot, while all the countries of the earth glide past us." And it was wonderful to behold how the whole coast moved. First came the lofty snow-capped Alps, overhung with clouds and overgrown with fir-trees. The horn was sounding its melancholy notes, while the shepherd was caroling in the vale. Then banana-trees flung their drooping branches over the boat; coal-black swans swam on the water, and flowers and animals of the strangest description might be seen on the shore. This was New Holland, the fifth part of the world, that glided past, with a view of the blue mountains. One could hear the hymns of the priests and see the savages dancing to the sound of drums and trumpets made of bones. Egypt's pyramids reaching to the clouds, overturned columns and sphinxes, half buried in the sand, followed in their turn. The aurora borealis next shone upon the extinguished volcanoes of the north. These were fireworks that nobody could have imitated! The prince was delighted; and he saw a hundred times more than what we have mentioned.

"Can I remain here forever?" asked he.

"That depends on yourself," replied the fairy. "If you do not long for what is forbidden, you may stay here forever."

"I will not touch the apple on the Tree of Knowledge," said the prince; "here are thousands of fruits equally fine."

"Examine your own heart, and if you do not feel sufficient strength, return with the East Wind who brought you hither. He is now about to fly back, and will not appear again in this place for the next hundred years. The time would seem to you here to be only a hundred hours, but even that is a long span for temptation and sin. Every evening, on leaving you, I shall be obliged to say: 'Come with me!' I shall make a sign with my hand, yet you must stay away. If once you followed, your longing would increase at every step. You would then enter the hall where grows the Tree of Knowledge I sleep beneath its perfumed, drooping branches. You would bend over me, and I should be forced to smile. But if you pressed a kiss on my lips, then would the garden sink into the earth and be lost for you. The sharp winds of the desert would howl around you, the cold rain would trickle over your head, and sorrow and distress would fall to your lot."

"I will remain here," said the prince. And the East Wind kissed his forehead, saying, "Be firm, and then we shall meet again in a hundred years. Farewell! farewell!" And the East Wind spread his large wings, and they shone like the lightning in harvest time, or like the northern lights in a cold winter.

"Farewell! farewell!" sounded from the flowers and the trees. Storks and pelicans flew in long rows, like streaming ribbons to accompany him to the boundaries of the garden.

"We will now begin our dances," said the fairy. "At the close, when I'm dancing with you, and just as the sun is sinking, you will see me make a sign, and you will hear me say, 'Come with me.' But do not do it. For a hundred years shall I be obliged to repeat the same thing every evening; and each time when it is over will you gain fresh strength. In the end you'll cease to think about it. This evening will be the first time—and now you are warned."

The fairy then led him into a large room made of white transparent lilies. The yellow stamina in each flower pictured a little golden harp that yielded a sweet music partaking of the combined sounds of stringed instruments and the tones of the flute. Lovely girls with slender aerial figures, and dressed in lightest gauze, floated through the mazes of the dance, and sang of the delights of living and being immortal, and blooming forever in the Garden of the World.

The sun now set. The whole sky was one mass of gold that imparted the tints of the richest roses to the lilies; and the prince drank of the sparkling wine handed to him by the youngmaidens, and felt a bliss he had never before experienced. He saw the background of the ballroom now opening, and the Tree of Knowledge stood before him in such streams of light that his eyes were dazzled. The singing that rang in his ears was soft and lovely as his mother's voice, and it seemed as if she sang, "My child! my beloved child!"

The fairy then made him a sign with her eyes, and cried most sweetly: "Come with me! Come with me!" And he rushed towards her, forgetting his promise, though it was but the first evening, and she continued to beckon to him and to smile. The spicy perfumes around grew yet more intoxicating; the harps sounded sweeter; and it was as if the millions of smiling faces in the room, where grew the tree, nodded and sang: "We must know everything! Man is the lord of the earth!" And there were no more tears of blood dropping down from the leaves of the Tree of Knowledge; but he thought he saw red sparkling stars instead.

"Come with me! come with me!" said the thrilling tones; and at each step the prince's cheeks glowed more intensely, and his blood rushed more wildly.

"I must!" said he; "it is no sin, and cannot be one! Why not follow when beauty calls? I will see her asleep; and provided I do not kiss her, there will be no harm done—and kiss I will not, for I have strength to resist, and a firm will."

And the fairy cast aside her dazzling attire, bent back the boughs, and in another moment was completely concealed.

"I have not yet sinned," said the prince, "and do not intend to sin!" And then he pushed the boughs aside; there she lay already asleep, and lovely as only the fairy of the Garden of the World is privileged to be. She smiled in her dreams; yet as he bent over her, he saw tears trembling between her eyelashes.

"And do you weep for me?" whispered he. "Oh, weep not, most admirable of women! I now begin to understand the happiness to be found in this place. It penetrates into my blood, and I feel the joys of the blessed in this my earthly form! Though it were ever after eternally dark for me, one moment like this is happiness enough!" And he kissed the tears in her eyes, and his mouth pressed her lips.

Then came a thunder-clap, so loud and so tremendous as never was heard before. Down everything fell to ruins — the beautiful fairy, the blooming garden, all sank deeper and deeper still. The prince saw the garden sinking into the dark abyss below, and it soon only shone like a little star in the distance. He turned as cold as death, and closed his eyes, and lay senseless.

The cold rain fell on his face, and the sharp wind blew over his head. He then returned to consciousness. "What have I done?" sighed he. "Alas! I have sinned, and the Island of Happiness has sunk down into the earth!" And he opened his eyes and saw a distant star like that of the sinking garden; but it was the morning star in the sky.

He got up and found himself in the large forest close to the Cavern of the Winds. The mother of the Winds sat by him, and looked angry, and raised her arm aloft.

"The very first evening," said she. "I thought it would be so! If you were my son, you should be put into the bag presently."

"Into it he shall go, sure enough!" said Death. He was a stalwart man with a scythe in his hand, and large black wings. "In his coffin shall he be laid, but not yet. I'll only mark him now, and allow him to wander about the world yet awhile, to expiate his sins and to grow better. But I shall come at last. When he least expects it, I shall put him into the black bag, place it on my head, and fly up to the stars.

There, too, blooms a lovely garden, and if he be good and pious, he will be allowed to enter it; but should his thoughts be wicked, and his heart still full of sin, then will he sink in his coffin yet lower than he saw the Garden of the World sink down; and it will be only once in every thousand years that I shall go and fetch him, when he will either be condemned to sink still deeper, or be borne aloft to the beaming stars above."

Milton Keynes UK
Ingram Content Group UK Ltd.
UKHW040652120923
428521UK00004B/232